COMEBACK

PETER CORRIS is known as the 'godfather' of Australian crime fiction through his Cliff Hardy detective stories. He has written in many other areas, including a co-authored autobiography of the late Professor Fred Hollows, a history of boxing in Australia, spy novels, historical novels and a collection of short stories about golf (see www.petercorris.net). In 2009, Peter Corris was awarded the Ned Kelly Award for Best Fiction by the Crime Writers Association of Australia. He is married to writer Jean Bedford and has lived in Sydney for most of his life. They have three daughters and five grandsons.

Peter Corris's thirty-seven Cliff Hardy books include *The Empty Beach*, *Master's Mates*, *The Coast Road*, *Saving Billie*, *The Undertow*, *Appeal Denied*, *The Big Score*, *Open File*, *Deep Water*, *Torn Apart*, *Follow the Money* and *Comeback*.

PETER CORRIS
COMEBACK

ALLEN&UNWIN
SYDNEY•MELBOURNE•AUCKLAND•LONDON

Thanks to Jean Bedford, Ruth Corris and Jo Jarrah.

First published in 2012

Allen & Unwin
Sydney, Melbourne, Auckland, London

83 Alexander Street
Crows Nest NSW 2065
Australia
Phone: (61 2) 8425 0100
Fax: (61 2) 9906 2218
Email: info@allenandunwin.com
Web: www.allenandunwin.com

Cataloguing-in-Publication details are available
from the National Library of Australia
www.trove.nla.gov.au

ISBN 978 1 74237 724 7

Internal text design by Emily O'Neill
Set in 12/17 pt Adobe Caslon by Midland Typesetters, Australia
Printed and bound in Australia by Griffin Press

'Atlantic City'—words and music by Bruce Springsteen
© Bruce Springsteen Music administered in Australia & New Zealand by Universal Music Publishing Pty Ltd. All rights reserved. International copyright secured. Reprinted with permission.

10 9 8 7 6 5 4 3 2

MIX
Paper from
responsible sources
FSC® C009448
www.fsc.org

The paper in this book is FSC® certified. FSC® promotes environmentally responsible, socially beneficial and economically viable management of the world's forests.

For Michael Wilding

A boxer makes a comeback for two reasons:
either he's broke or he needs the money.

Alan 'Boom' Minter, British boxer

part one

1

'You read the papers don't you, Cliff?' my lawyer, Viv Garner, said.

'All depends,' I said.

'On what?'

'Whether they're going to make me angry or not, and a lot of things make me angry—politics, economics, religion, television . . .'

'That just about covers it. Bit sour though.'

'Oh, a lot of things make me happy. Make me laugh. Sometimes the same things that make me angry. I'm not sour. You might say bittersweet.'

'Okay, I gather you haven't followed the High Court decision in the case of Wade versus the Commissioner of Police.'

We were drinking coffee in a place in Glebe Point Road that had been recommended to me by a coffee snob. 'The best, mate,' he'd said. It was okay, better than some, and they'd served it very hot, the way I like it. Viv had rung wanting to meet and offering to buy. He knew I was broke or very close to it. I'd ordered a croissant to go with the coffee. I'd been skipping meals a bit to save money. I thought I could probably tap Viv for a second cup. I shook my head in answer to his question.

'Jack Wade was, and will be again possibly, a licensed commercial and private inquiry agent. Like you, the Commissioner banned him for life.'

That got my interest. 'What did he do?'

'He impersonated a police officer for financial gain. The thing is, a law firm took up the case and fought it all the way to the High Court. The court decided that life bans are unconstitutional. Violation of human rights.'

'What's the upshot?'

'Jack wins the right to apply for a review of his case to the Security Industry Registry. If he gets the nod there it's likely the Commission'll have to settle for a suspension, say, three years.'

I forgot about coffee good or bad, hot or cold. 'I've done more than that already.'

Viv's smile was smug. 'Exactly.' He reached into his briefcase. 'I downloaded the appropriate forms. Does that make you happy?'

'I think it might. You want a kiss?'

'No thanks. I just want to see you back at work.'

■ ■ ■

It happened and more easily than I'd imagined. I'd had a couple of suspensions even before I'd had the book thrown at me. I'd served a brief gaol term which, strictly speaking, should have cancelled me out for a long spell except that I had some high-profile help. There was no chance of getting help this time. The application was processed and the hearing was held and the matter was referred to a committee and a sub-committee and they must have built up a metre-high stack of paper. But in the end I was reinstated, given the plastic licence card and a folder of rules and regulations that would have taken a week to read.

Then it was a matter of getting liability insurance at a ruinous rate given my age and record, joining a gun club and putting in the hours to qualify for a pistol licence and renting an office and furniture. All costly. I'd had my house in Glebe free and clear of mortgage for years; now I took out a sizeable mortgage again at a high interest rate over the fairly short term the bank allowed me. Gratifying, though, to find out what the old place was worth. I felt I'd got away with something. I was back in business with a necessity to earn money to cover my overheads. Just like the old days and I got a lift from it.

At my daughter Megan's insistence I bought some new clothes, and that gave me a buzz, too. But I drew the line at changing cars; Megan just wanted to get her hands on my noble old Falcon.

The office was in Pyrmont, squeezed between Miller Street and Bridge Road. The building had been a warehouse. It'd been gutted, honeycombed, painted and rewired but sometimes I could swear I still smelled wool or wheat or copra or whatever had been stored there. I threw a small office-warming party. Megan, her partner Hank and my ten-month-old grandson Ben, Frank and Hilde Parker, Viv Garner, Daphne Rowley, my doctor Ian Sangster and a few other Glebe types drank cask red and white, ate saladas and cheese slices and wished me luck.

'Fresh start, Cliff,' Frank Parker, who'd retired as a Deputy Commissioner of Police, said as he examined my secondhand Mac and phone and fax set-up. 'Not common at your age. How're you feeling?'

'Bit anxious but optimistic,' I said. 'Comebacks aren't such a good idea, even if Ali made it.'

Frank nodded. 'He stayed at it too long though.'

'I'll know pretty quickly whether I've still got it,' I said. 'In this game you've got the knack or you haven't. Anyway, I have to give it a go. Trouble is, I'm out of touch with the usual conduits, the lawyers and such.'

Daphne Rowley, who runs a printing business and plays pool with me at the Toxteth Hotel, topped up her plastic glass with the red. 'That's why I got him to advertise, Frank,' she said. 'Ads in the local rags, cards up here and there and a website.'

Frank almost spilled his drink. '*You*, a website?'

'Megan set it up,' I said. 'Photo makes me look ten years younger.'

'It'd need to,' Frank said. 'Well, good luck, mate, and try to stay out of trouble. They'll be keeping an eye on you.'

I'd worried about the website and the photograph. In the past anonymity had been the PIA's stock in trade but times had changed. If you're not in cyberspace you're nowhere. Anyway, the photo didn't look all that much like me.

They drifted off and I shovelled the glasses and paper plates and uneaten food into a garbag. I sat at the desk and examined the room. It felt better for having had people and wine and talk in it. Less sterile. But the brightness and the clean surfaces made me uncomfortable. My two battered filing cabinets and the bar fridge from offices past stood against the wall like comfortable old friends. The hired desk and chairs weren't new either and I noticed a couple of wine stains on the pale grey carpet. I'd soon knock the place into shape.

I sat there wondering if I'd made the right decision. The private inquiry business has changed radically over the past decade or so. Now it's all search engines and databases and emails and very little knocking on doors. I'm told some people in the game charge by the hour, like lawyers. I was always one for getting out there, asking around, finding the pressure points and applying the force. Of course I did my share of bodyguarding and money minding, but there were security firms doing those jobs exclusively now. Process serving could provide a steady but minor income stream like credit checking. But credit checking in particular was completely computerised now. The question was, were there still human problems out there that needed the personal touch, the right question, the accumulated experience of more than twenty years? I was sure there must be.

The mortgage didn't worry me too much. There it was, an extraction from a slender bank account every month with heavy penalties for failing to have enough money to cover it. I decided to see it as a stimulus. Until about eighteen months before, I'd enjoyed a period of affluence, courtesy of an inheritance from my partner, Lily Truscott. I hadn't exactly enjoyed it; I felt guilty about it mostly, and it had all gone west in a financial scam of which I was the victim. It'd been a bad feeling and I'd done things about it. That had primed me for my new start. I was ready.

I kept busy renewing old contacts and trying to establish new ones. A few crackpots approached me—a psychic offering her services, a wannabe crime writer with twenty rejected manuscripts wanting me to read them and tell him where he went wrong, a defrocked minister wanting me to prove that the woman who had replaced him was an atheist. One matter I had to look at very seriously. It was a thinly veiled invitation to shoot a witness in a criminal trial. It had a peculiar smell to it and I concluded that it was a set-up, either by the police or some old enemy, designed to put me deep in the shit. Big bait, but I didn't bite.

The doubt was pretty much dispelled when Robert 'Bobby' Forrest turned up to keep the appointment he'd made by phone. Forrest was tall and lean, say 188 centimetres and 80 kilos. He was also remarkably handsome, with fair hair and regular features. Good teeth. His knock lacked authority though, and he was clearly nervous as he took a seat.

'My father recommended you, Mr Hardy,' he said.

I sighed. The generation gap with a vengeance. Forrest was in his mid-twenties at a guess. That probably put his dad in his fifties.

'Who would that be?'

'Ray Frost. I changed my name for professional reasons. Dad said you handled a delicate matter for him way back when. He said he thought you'd gone out of business, but I found your web page.'

'I took a break. I'm sorry, I don't remember the name Ray Frost. Did he tell you what it was about?'

He shook his head. 'He wouldn't say. He was a bit of a wild man back then, I gather.'

'Probably best to leave it then. Anyway, I'm glad I gave satisfaction. What can I do for you?'

I have misgivings about grown men using a diminutive like Bobby, but it happens and probably more in show business than anywhere else. He was wearing sneakers, jeans, a T-shirt and a leather jacket. All good quality and expensive-looking. He fiddled with the zip on the jacket. 'It's like, kind of embarrassing.'

I nodded the way the psychiatrists do, trying to look comforting as well as professionally concerned.

'I'm being stalked.' He blurted it out.

Another nod. 'By whom?'

'I . . . sort of . . . don't know.'

He had my attention. A changed name and a mysterious stalker will do that every time. I must have got the comforting look right because he stopped fidgeting, sat up straight and told me the story.

Bobby Forrest was an actor. He'd changed his name because Frost had connotations of cold and discomfort, and Forrest suggested something natural and, in these greening days, valuable. He said he'd dropped out of NIDA and hadn't regretted it. A good part had come along and he'd grabbed it and been in regular work ever since, in television, films and commercials. He wasn't surprised when I admitted I'd never heard of him.

'No offence,' he said, 'but I'm geared towards a younger market.'

'Fair enough,' I said. 'Very wise.'

'I'm pretty well known. I've done a lot of TV and some movies. I've been on the cover of a few magazines and stuff like that. But I know I'm not that smart,' he said.

I made the sort of gesture you make but he was serious. He said he'd been good at a variety of sports at school. He could sing and dance a bit and play a couple of musical instruments, but he'd never been interested in studying and his talent for acting was just a knack. He'd always liked to show off. He planned to start reading books and developing his mind.

'I've got a girlfriend who's helping me with that. Her name's Jane. I've got a photo . . .' He started to reach for the inside pocket of his jacket but stopped. 'I'm getting ahead of myself. I haven't been much of a success with girls—shy, really. So I tried the online dating thing and that's how I met Jane. But before I met her I got into a sort of online relationship with this other woman.'

He took two photos from his jacket and studied them. 'I don't know if you know how online dating works, Mr Hardy.'

'Call me Cliff. I've got a rough idea. You exchange information and photos and if you tick enough boxes with each other you arrange to meet.'

'That's right. With no obligation on either side. If you don't get along, all bets are off with no harm done.'

Just stating it so matter-of-factly made me see a whole minefield. No obligation, the bet's off, no harm done, can mean very different things to different people.

He selected one of the photos and put it on my desk as if he was glad to be rid of it. It was a full-length shot of an extremely attractive woman. She was slim and dark, provocatively posed in a tight dress that showed an impressive length of shapely leg.

Forrest held the other photo as though it was fragile or so light it might float away. He pointed to the photo on the desk.

'I met her once. You don't have to use your real names. I didn't use mine. She said her name was Miranda but it probably wasn't. She said she was an actress.'

'It didn't take?'

'She was awful. Very conceited and aggressive. Tried to . . . run everything. It was a disaster and I couldn't get away quick enough.'

It was mid-October and getting warm outside. He was dressed a bit too heavily in the leather jacket but it was the memory of his meeting with Miranda that was making him sweat. He transferred the photo to his left hand and rubbed his fist across his damp forehead.

'Sorry,' he said. 'Like I say, it was awful . . . in every way. I thought that was it and I went back online, looking, and I found Jane. We met and hit it off right away. She's terrific. She's very smart, much smarter than me, but she somehow makes me feel smarter than I am, better than I am, if you can understand that.'

I wasn't sure, but I thought I could. 'A good feeling.'

'The best. But this other one, she won't leave me alone. She bombards me with text messages and emails. She's turned up a few times at places where I've been. I've no idea how she finds out my movements. I get the feeling that I'm being followed sometimes, but that might just be paranoia—isn't that what they call it?'

'Yes. Does Jane know about her?'

'No, and that's one of my worries. Jane is sort of insecure about me.'

'How's that?'

He shook his head. 'It's hard to explain and it's bound up with one of my other problems. The whole fucking thing's all bound up together and with my . . . I'm sorry, Mr . . . Cliff, I'm not sure I can go on with this.'

It was 4 pm, late enough under the circumstances. I had a bottle of Black Douglas in the bottom drawer of the desk. I got it out, opened the bar fridge and put a couple of ice cubes in two plastic glasses left over from the party. I added solid slugs of the scotch and pushed the drink across to him.

'Have a drink, Bobby, and collect your thoughts. Nothing you say to me gets said to anyone else without your permission.'

He took the glass and had a sip, then a longer pull. 'Okay, thanks. This is the really embarrassing bit . . . bits. Being stalked by a woman and not being able to handle it, that's bad enough, but . . . I went home with Miranda. I don't know why. I suppose I thought I should. I couldn't get it up for her. She was beautiful and all that, but I just couldn't. I've had some trouble in that department over the years . . .'

'You're not Robinson Crusoe.'

'What? Oh, yeah, but nothing like this. It was miserable.'

'Do I have to ask the obvious question?'

'No. With Jane everything is wonderful. Amazing, really. But Miranda, or whoever she is, has threatened to harm Jane. To physically hurt her. And she says she'll tell her I'm really gay and that I'm just using her as a . . .'

'Beard, the Americans call it.'

'Do they? Okay. She says she knows I'm not and that she can fix my problem, but she says she's so hurt that's what she'd do.'

'Unless?'

'Unless I agree to see her, respond to her messages and emails, go on a holiday with her, all that.'

'These threats come how?'

'Emails, letters, cards, phone calls.'

He handed me the other photograph. It showed a young woman sitting in a chair smiling shyly at the camera. She had curly, cropped hair, a pug nose and slightly droopy eyes. She wore a blouse and a skirt that covered her knees. Forrest cleared his throat.

'Jane isn't beautiful, as you can see, but that doesn't matter to me. She's wonderful and I love her, but because I look the way I do . . . shit, I hate saying this.'

'She feels she's not good enough for you while you feel you're not good enough for her.'

He had large, expressive blue eyes like Mel Gibson and he

opened them wide. 'That's it exactly. I can't bear the thought of losing her or of any harm coming to her because of me.'

'Tell me about the threats to Jane.'

'They're kind of veiled, I suppose you'd call it. Nothing like "I'll throw acid in her face" or like that. But she says how people can have accidents, how they can contract diseases by being in the wrong place at the wrong time. She says she knows people who can arrange things and how Sydney is such a dangerous city.'

'Nothing direct?'

'No.'

'And you believe she's capable of carrying out these threats?'

'That's the trouble, I don't know. But I can't afford to take the risk. I'm embarrassed about all this. The only person I've been able to talk to about it was my dad. Can you help me?'

2

It didn't feel like such a big deal. It was a reversal of the usual stalker scenario, but what could I expect? It was the twenty-first century and we had climate change, an unwinnable war supported by both sides of politics, a minority government and a female prime minister. Change was everywhere.

Bobby said he'd been back to Miranda's flat but she wasn't there. He felt too angry to reply to her emails or phone calls because he was worried she might record him saying something he shouldn't. He mentioned his bad temper. He wanted me to find Miranda and talk to her. Persuade her that the course she was following would only get her into serious trouble.

'Would you take legal action?'

He finished his drink as he thought about it. 'I'd be reluctant. It'd be embarrassing and Jane would find out all about it. But Dad says you're good at getting through to people. If you thought she was serious about the threats and wouldn't listen, then yes, I'd take legal action.'

That was sensible. He was smarter than he thought. I had him sign a contract and pay over a retainer. I asked him for more details on how the particular dating website he'd used worked and he filled me in. I took notes. I got his email address and his postal address, his landline and his mobile number.

Jane's surname was Devereaux and I got her details, including the publishing company she worked for as a commissioning editor. I got Bobby's agent's details and those for his father. Bobby and I shook hands and he thanked me effusively. So far all he'd had was a sympathetic ear, and the retainer he'd given me, in line with what I'd learned was the new scale of fees, was steep. I felt I had to have something to contribute immediately. I asked him if Miranda had given him a deadline for carrying out her threats.

'Not exactly, but she implied I didn't have long.'

'If I have trouble finding her, another way might be for you to contact her and arrange to meet. I could step in then.'

He looked dismayed at the prospect, almost angry when I told him that if it came to making contact with Miranda it would be better to do it by phone in case Jane read his emails.

'She wouldn't do that.'

'You never know what a person will do.'

The anger subsided. A flush had come over his face and he'd gripped the arms of his chair so that the structure creaked. He drew in a deep breath. 'I don't think I could meet her. I think if I did I might . . .'

'Do what?'

He shook his head and didn't answer.

'How strong is this feeling of being followed?'

'Pretty strong. I haven't known what to do about it with Jane there in case it was Miranda herself. I mean, she talked about knowing people . . .'

He was suddenly anxious to go and I let him. I stared at the closed door and wondered what he'd been going to say. Was it, *I might try to prove my manhood*, or *I might harm her?*

After he left I scanned my notes and the signed contract into the computer and created a file for it. I scanned the photos of Miranda and Jane into the computer and made copies. Then I threw the notes away. They say the paperless office didn't happen; I kept the signed contract but otherwise I was prepared to get as close to paperless as I could.

I checked the site Bobby had used. The drill was to choose a username which could include a bit of your real name or not. The instructions suggested that it was a good idea to give a hint of your main interests at this stage. Then you set up a profile with a list of your interests, likes and dislikes. At this point you also sketch in the kind of person you're looking for. You get an 'inbox' so people can send you messages through the site and you can respond to them. No email address or contact details until you get responses and have communicated back and forth enough to feel confident you've latched on to a 'possible'. Then contact details and face-to-face meetings are up to you. Photographs are optional in the profile but you can protect them from being looked at by all and sundry and restrict access to them to people who take your fancy. You can pay a subscription, and Bobby's was pretty heavy, or just buy credits and pay message by message.

Bobby, looking shamefaced, had told me that Miranda's photograph had attracted him and her list of interests included acting and several sports he was keen on. He'd 'messaged' her, got a response and they communicated a few times before arranging a meeting at a wine bar in Coogee. He'd given her his email address and mobile number. Once bitten, he'd been more cautious with Jane and they'd spent more time providing details and filling in backgrounds before they'd arranged to meet. He said he hadn't been disappointed by her looks when they met at a coffee shop in Randwick. He described her face as fascinating. She hadn't objected to his intellectual shortcomings. He said they'd laughed a lot and at the same sorts of things. He'd agreed to read some books and she'd agreed to let him teach her to play golf. They went to bed on their third meeting and hit the jackpot.

It all sounded potentially very dangerous to me unless you played strictly by the rules and exercised a great deal of common sense. But I suppose that applied to the old style of meetings between the sexes. How many mistakes had I made in connecting up with women and how many women had made mistakes in connecting up with me?

First things first. I had to know more about Bobby Forrest. His website was just a photo, a few broad-brush details and a list of his film and TV credits. I'd never heard of the films or the television shows. His agent, Sophie Marjoram, I did know from back when I did security work for film crews. I rang her and arranged to meet her the following morning. That left me sitting in the office at 6 pm with a paying client, a glass of scotch and a nagging half-memory. When I focused on it the name Ray Frost rang a bell but nothing more. Over the years I've done favours for people that haven't needed a documentary record. I guess everybody has. If the name had cropped up in that context I'd have to rely on my uncertain memory, but I had a feeling that it was something more than that.

My filing system has never been well organised and, what with moving office a couple of times and a spell of working from home, it'd become a bit chaotic. So it took me more than an hour and another drink to track down Ray Frost. It was twenty-five years ago. All it took was a glance at one of the notes I'd made to bring the whole thing back to me.

Frost had been in gaol, on remand for involvement in an armed robbery.

'He's innocent,' Frost's lawyer, Charles Bickford, had told me. 'I want you to prove it.'

It was a bit unusual for a lawyer to be so adamant about the innocence of a client and I asked Bickford why he thought so.

'The police have it in for him. He's been in trouble before and he's a maverick sort of character. Won't take shit from anyone, including me. I can't help liking him.'

I'd dealt with Bickford before and more or less trusted his judgement, so I took his money and the case. Three men had robbed an armoured car delivery to a business in the CBD very early in the morning. They'd been masked and were efficient. They didn't injure the guards and got away with about sixty thousand dollars—probably less than they'd expected. A witness said the mask on one of the robbers had slipped and he identified Frost in a lineup. I went to see Frost in Long Bay.

'It's bullshit,' he said. 'I was at home asleep. I've never worn a mask in my life.'

'How do you figure it, then?'

Frost was a big, solid man, handsome in a rugged way. He was very calm, which isn't easy to be when you're on remand facing a serious charge. I knew because I'd been there. He didn't fidget or avoid my eyes. He smoked, as so many did back then, including me, but not compulsively.

'Must've been someone who looked like me. Plenty do.'

That was true enough. He said he was alone in the house at the time of the robbery. His wife had just had a premature baby and was still in the hospital with it. He'd been awake for two days through the crisis and was grabbing some sleep.

'How d'you read it?' I asked.

'To be honest, I see it as payback. I'm no angel and the cops haven't managed to nail me for a few things I have done. They're causing me grief for something I didn't do.'

There were a lot of dodgy police back then, many of them capable of framing people and using their powers and the courts to pay old debts.

'What about the other two?'

He shrugged. 'No idea who those guys are but I could hazard a guess.'

'That might help.'

'No, I'm not a dog, but you know how it works, Hardy. They could've green-lighted the job and set me up to take the blame.'

He was right about that. It happened. If it had, the weak spot in the arrangement was the witness. I poked around and got enough on him for Bickford to cast serious doubt on his evidence if the case came to trial. It didn't. Wheels turned and the charges were dropped. It made me popular with Bickford, who put work my way for the next few years. Frost had thanked me. It made me unpopular with the police but that was nothing new.

The files were arranged in chronological order so I could see that other matters had come along hard on the heels of that one. It had been a busy time and the details had been crowded out long ago. I made some notes, put the old file back in its place, and copied the notes into the Forrest file and then to the memory stick. I fitted the memory stick onto my key ring. It felt like a day's work so that's what I called it.

I felt good about Bobby's case. It had an interesting texture to it. The phone rang as I was about to leave the office. It was Sarah Kelly, a woman I'd met down in the Illawarra on a brief holiday a while back.

'You said you'd call me,' she said.

'I should have,' I said.

'When are you likely to be down here again? I want to see you, Cliff.'

I realised that I wanted to see her, too. Badly. Being back at work and on something interesting was all very well, but I needed warmth. Viv had said I was sour. I didn't feel sour, especially when I heard Sarah's voice. She was a part-time soul singer and her voice had a special quality.

'I'm back in business, Sarah. It's great to hear from you.'

'Busy, eh, baby? Well get here soon.'

I went to the Toxteth in an uppish mood, didn't drink too much and Daphne Rowley and I held the pool table until our eyes got crossed.

Sophie Marjoram had an office in Paddington not far from the Five Ways. It was wedged between an art gallery and an antique dealer with a pub just across the street and a coffee shop half a block away. Ideal location. Sophie specialised in all aspects of the film and television business. She was an agent for writers, directors, actors, sound engineers, special effects people, stunt persons, you name it. It was a good niche that enabled her, sometimes, to get quite a few of her clients in on the one film or TV production and guarantee stability and reliability. And lock in good commissions for herself. She didn't have any of the big names.

'Don't want 'em,' she'd told me when I first met her. 'Nothing but ego, ego, ego. I've had a few on the way up who've left me when they made it, and come back to me on the way down. A microcosm of life's what it feels like sometimes.'

Our appointment was for 10 am. I showed up on time and she was late. She came hurrying along the street, high-heeled boots tapping, flowing skirt flapping and with a mobile phone glued to her ear. Still listening and talking she dug keys out of her bag, opened the door and waved me inside.

'Fuck you,' she said and switched off the phone.

'Another successful negotiation, Soph?'

'It will be, it will be.'

We went down a short passage to an open plan office holding three desks.

'You've expanded,' I said. 'You used to have half this space.'

'I'm doing okay. I've got two part-timers. I get a government subsidy for employing them, would you believe? You ought to be in on it.'

'I'm just starting up again after a break. Barely enough work for me so far.'

She sat behind the biggest, most cluttered desk and pointed to a chair.

'Good to see you, anyway. I guess one of my people must be in trouble. Who is it?'

Direct, that's Sophie, at least when she was sober, which wasn't always. She was in her fifties, overweight, vividly made up, energetic. She'd done most of the jobs she now handled as an agent herself in her time except for stunting, and she could be hard as nails or marshmallow soft as required.

'Bobby Forrest,' I said. 'Trouble not really of his own making.'

'It never is. Well, I know how it works. You won't tell me a thing about it, and I have to tell you everything I know about him.'

'Not quite like that. He hasn't committed any crimes, isn't a drunk or on drugs or a pedophile, as far as I know.'

'That's a relief. I can tell you that he's a good kid. Good actor, a natural. Limited range but he's working on that. In a way he's got too many skills. He can do just about anything and the producers use him a lot, but in snatches, if you know what I mean. He's yet to get any good, solid roles but he keeps busy.'

'How bright is he?'

'How bright are any of them? Not very.'

I showed Sophie the photograph of Miranda and asked

if she'd ever seen her. She put on glasses and studied it carefully.

'Chocolate box,' she said. 'No, don't know her.'

'Is Forrest, let's say . . . prone to violence?'

'Ah, now we're getting to it, are we? It's not what he's done, it's what he might do.'

'You're talking. Go on.'

Sophie fiddled with the pens and pencils standing up in a jar on her desk. She selected one and ran her fingers along its length. It had an eraser at the end and she used it to bounce the pencil on the desk.

'As far as I know, Cliff,' she said slowly, weighing her words, 'you're one of the good guys, although your record doesn't quite show that, I'm told. You've cut some corners, trodden on some toes.'

I nodded. 'Corners that needed cutting, toes that needed treading on.'

'You always did a good job for me, sometimes under difficult circumstances. You could've picked up money talking juicy stuff to the media.'

I didn't say anything.

'So I'm going to trust you.'

'Yes?'

She laughed. 'Had you going, didn't I? You thought I was going to reveal some deep, dark secret about Bobby.'

'Well?'

'No, there's nothing. He is what he seems to be.'

Sophie had been an actress but apparently not a very good one. I thought she was acting now, but I couldn't be sure in what kind of role. That's the trouble with theatrical people. When are they acting and when are they being straight? If ever, either way?

'Come on, Soph. Is there something?'

'No, nothing.'

I simply didn't know whether to believe her or not and I let it go. We talked a bit more. I thanked her and left her still stroking and bouncing her pencil. In books and movies the private eye seeking information lurks outside the door to listen to the subject pick up the phone and give the game away. I'd never done it and, anyway, in Sophie's office there was nowhere to lurk.

The simplest way of meeting up with Miranda, if it worked, was to check whether she was following Bobby. I rang him on his mobile.

'This is Cliff Hardy, Bobby. Where are you?'

'I'm out at Fox Studios doing some voice-overs.'

'What're your plans for the rest of the day?'

'I'm going to play a round at Anzac Park with a mate and then go home and read and then pick up Jane and go out to eat. Why?'

'I want to check whether you're being followed.'

I got a description of his car and the registration number.

He told me where he was parked and how long before he'd be back at his car. I told him not to worry about feeling he was being followed because I'd be doing it.

He laughed. 'Well, that'll be a new experience. What will you do if someone else *is* following me?'

He sounded much more relaxed than before, perhaps too relaxed. It happens sometimes. People feel better for just having talked the problem over and being offered some help, still to be delivered. It's like the way an ailment can feel better after you decide to see a doctor.

I had time to get out to what used to be the showgrounds and take up a position within sight of Bobby's red Alfa Romeo. Right car for a rising star. It was Tuesday and quiet at the complex. I spotted the Alfa and parked in a two-hour zone close by. Bobby came out within a couple of minutes of the time he'd suggested. He was dressed pretty much as before but carrying a slim briefcase. He opened the car from fifty metres away and looked around, but there were twenty or thirty cars parked in the area and he didn't know which was mine. He tossed the briefcase onto the back seat, climbed in and drove away. I waited to see if any of the parked cars would follow him. None did.

He drove fast, too fast and aggressively for the amount of traffic. He cut in and out, skilfully but leaving little margin for error. After one manoeuvre the car he'd cut in on gave him a blast on the horn and tailgated him up to a set of lights. Bobby jumped out and strode back to the car. The other driver got out and stretched a 190-plus centimetre body with bulk to match. Bobby shouted at him and the driver shaped up to throw a punch. Bobby got ready to mix it. Cars were banked up at the lights and horns were blaring. I was two cars back. I got out and shouted.

'Police!'

Bobby and the other man froze. I came up and jostled Bobby.

'I'm not a cop, but look around. Half these people are on their mobiles and the cops'll be here any minute. You two fuckwits better get back in your cars and piss off.'

The pair looked around. The big guy shrugged and got back in his car. Bobby did the same and drove off, just catching the green light. He'd mentioned his bad temper and now I'd seen an example of it. Pretty extreme. You could say it added shading to his rather bland character, but it was a dangerous addition.

I followed, hanging back, made the short run to the golf course and pulled into the car park. A Mazda pulled in next to him. A young man got out and shook hands with Bobby. They hauled their clubs and buggies out of their cars and squatted on the driver's seats with the door open to change their shoes. Then they fitted the clubs to the buggies and strolled away. I rang his mobile. Golfers tell me you need a clear head, preferably an empty one, to play well. I wondered if Bobby was still seeing red.

'Hardy,' I said. 'Jesus, Bobby, you need to watch your temper. That guy would've flattened you.'

He sounded calm. 'I know. I'm sorry. It's a problem.'

'I'd say so. Anyway, you're all clear for now. Enjoy your round. What time will you leave home to pick up Jane?'

He told me. That left me with eight empty hours. I drove back to Pyrmont and entered a few notes on my conversation with Sophie Marjoram into the Forrest file. I Googled Goldstein Smith Publishing and clicked on the name Jane Devereaux. The entry came up with another photograph, just an upper body shot showing her at her desk, and a list of her accomplishments. It was a formidable tally—honours degree and a Masters in comparative literature, a batch of literary criticism articles published, co-editorship of a literary magazine. The photograph showed her glancing up in the direction of the lens. The shy smile was there along with an expression that could only be called intelligent. It enlivened her face but left it a long way short of pretty. I wondered about the attraction between her and Bobby. On the surface it looked like an attraction of opposites, but that was probably too simple. I copied the entry and added it to the file. Still no more paper.

Sophie had given me the names of a few films Bobby had been in and I found three in my local DVD place. Action stuff mostly. Looked watchable.

I had lunch in a café and went to the Redgum Gym in Leichhardt to work off the lunch. Since my heart attack and bypass I've had to take quite a bit of medication and some of it has to be taken clear of food and clear of other medication.

It irritates me having to swallow pills at particular times, but not as much as another bypass would. I put in a solid workout on the treadmill, the machines and the free weights and felt virtuous.

'Going fine, Cliff,' Wesley Scott, the proprietor, said as I completed the last set. 'Looking more cheerful too, man.'

'I'm back in business, Wes.'

'God help us. So you'll be coming in all bruised and battered again.'

'No, I'm aiming for a better class of client.'

'Won't be hard to achieve. How's your grandson?'

'Thriving. How's business?'

'Would you believe I've signed up five politicians all keen to lose weight and look good for the next election.'

'Which side?'

'Both sides, man. Both sides.'

'Must be hard to tell them apart.'

Bobby lived in Redfern in a street that was physically close to the Block, the area heavily populated by Aborigines, and a continual problem for people well disposed to the Aborigines and those hostile to them. But Bobby's street was a million miles away in economic terms. Every house in it had been gentrified recently and the speed humps were new and the bricked footpath was even newer. It was on the fringes of Surry Hills and it was a sure bet the real estate agents advertised the houses as 'suit Surry Hills buyer' just as they used to say 'suit Balmain buyer' for overpriced ruins in the inner-west.

Bobby's house was a neat, single-storey terrace. Good investment if he owned it, high rent if he didn't. The Alfa was parked outside and I had about half an hour until Bobby emerged, slamming the door behind him and feeling in his jacket for the keys. He was more smartly dressed than before—white shirt, beige jacket, dark slacks, boots. I was parked just around the corner in a cross street. Not many of the houses had driveways and there were quite a few cars parked in the street. Bobby drove off, heading east, and no one followed except me.

He drove carefully and well, more like a solid citizen than a speedway performer this time. Maybe he'd learned his lesson or perhaps the thought of Jane had a calming influence on him, or perhaps it was just because he knew I was following him. I kept a few cars back. It's easy to follow someone when you know where they're going and Bobby was obviously heading to Randwick, where Jane lived. Her street was off Alison Road, not far from the racecourse. Bobby pulled up outside a block of flats and used his mobile phone. No honking horns or knocking on doors these days. There was nowhere to park, he'd snaffled the last spot in the street, so I had to cruise past, turn and come back. It took two passes before Jane came out of the building. Bobby sprang from the car and wrapped his arms around her. She was smaller than she appeared in the photograph and she virtually disappeared into his big-bodied hug.

They broke apart and he opened the car door for her. She wore high heels, a dark-coloured pants suit and a white blouse. It was a simple but elegant outfit, not striving for glamour. Well, it was only Wednesday night. They did some kissing before Bobby started the car and moved off. I was going slowly in the other direction. A Commodore that had been parked fifty metres from the Alfa started up and followed it—at least it made the same turn, further down the street. I lost time and distance going in the wrong direction before I could turn. I got back as quickly as I could and saw the Commodore waiting to make the turn into Alison Road.

The traffic was heavy and the Commodore had to bluff its way into the stream of traffic and I had to do the same. The Alfa had to be a fair distance ahead and it was no certainty yet that the Commodore was following it. The road rose and although the light was dropping I could see the Alfa signalling right in the distance. The Commodore nearly caused an accident getting across to make the turn. I was locked into a stream of traffic and there was no way I could change lanes. The Alfa and the Commodore headed off and I was forced to carry on a kilometre or more before I could make my way back.

There was a maze of streets in the direction they'd taken

and any number of options for dinner. A waste of time trying to track them. I was certain that Bobby had been followed and equally certain that Miranda wasn't doing the following. Not unless she was a mistress of disguise—the driver of the Commodore had been a man.

3

There's a lot of waiting and time killing in this game, always has been. I had a meal and a glass of red in a pub near the racecourse, walked around for a bit and then squeezed into a barely legal parking spot close to Jane's block of flats. If the car that had followed Bobby showed up again I'd get another chance to follow it. Didn't happen. The Alfa returned and Bobby drove into the block's parking area. Looked as though Jane had parking rights Bobby could use. I stayed put and a light came on in a corner flat on the second floor. Two figures came out onto the balcony and merged into one figure. I drove home feeling more than a touch of envy at their closeness. I'd had my share of assignations and I missed the feeling they can give you. I told myself I was just in a pause, not retired.

My house seemed even emptier and more lonely than it usually did. Megan was urging me to sell it, get something more cheerful, more manageable. She was right but I had trouble with the idea. I'd had the house a long time, ever since my marriage to Cyn, and it was imbued with memories, some bad, mostly good. I'd made love there, spilt blood and had some of my own spilt. There's been times when I was flush with money and other times, like now, when funds were low. I knew I should find a way to shake all this loose and go somewhere else, but I was back in business and somehow that seemed to make keeping the house and the memories all the more important.

I went through all this with a large scotch to wash down my night-time medications. Not exactly the doctors' recommendation, but I resented taking the pills so much I needed some compensation. My thoughts drifted back to the Bobby Forrest case and I told myself I'd made some progress. Hard to say what conclusions to draw, but that wasn't unusual this early in the piece. I'd turned on many more lights than I needed to work against the emptiness of the house and I promised myself I'd stop doing that. Now I went through turning them off. The power bill would be colossal if I kept it up and I wasn't afraid of the dark.

I phoned Bobby the next morning to tell him he had been followed, but by a man.

'A man? Well, she said she knew people.'

'Right. Are you going to be out and about today?'

'Yeah, I've got a meeting with a producer at ten, a lunch with some friends and then I thought I'd drive out to where they're going to be shooting my next film. Just to take a look.'

'Where's that?'

'Parramatta. I have to do a river swim there and I want to get a look at the spot. Swimming in rivers can be tricky. Haven't been out there for a while.'

'Do you do your own stunts?'

'Mostly. It's fun.'

'What? Falling from high buildings?'

He laughed. 'No, I leave that to the experts. But things like swimming and fight scenes. I like them—you have to get the timing just right.'

No doubt, I thought. The last thing he'd want would be a broken nose. I'd got the timing wrong a few times in the real thing.

'Jane again tonight?'

'No, she's busy. What she calls the slush pile.'

'Okay. I don't want to alarm you, but if you see a white Commodore on your trail, keep driving for as long as you can. Circle back towards the city and call me. I'll try to catch up with you.'

'A white Commodore. Okay.'

'Don't be heroic if you spot it. Just call me.'

'What will you be doing, Cliff?'

'Finding Miranda. If I can.'

I could hear the relief in his voice. 'That might mean I won't have to contact her.'

'Might.'

I was tired of thinking about the name Miranda as if it was in inverted commas. Bobby had told me he'd mostly communicated with her via the dating site and by mobile but that he'd had some emails from her. I asked him to forward them to me before he went about his business for the day.

'They're embarrassing,' he said.

'Just do it, please. I need to get a feel for her style.'

'I gave you her address.'

'You gave me *an* address. How do you know it was really where she lived? She might've been playing it cautious on a first date. I bet you didn't tell her where you lived that time.'

'You're right. Shit, I wish I'd never ... All right, I'll forward the bloody emails now.'

Not the smoothest conversation with a client, but I needed his involvement. I drove into Pyrmont, bought a takeaway long black and went up to the office. The mail box was half full of 'to the occupier' junk with only a couple of bills directed specifically at me. I'd given Bobby my bank details and when I checked online his payment was in, making the balance look temporarily respectable. My inbox held a message from Megan, one from the Dendy cinema telling me what was playing and what was coming up, and three forwarded from Bobby.

COMEBACK

My darling Bobby
I can't understand why you are treating me so cruel. You know
what a beautiful pair we make together. I have your picture up
everywhere in my place, in every room, so I can look at you all
the time. If you did the same I'm sure you'd feel as I do that we
belong together. Please don't make me so unhappy. She's not for
you, my love. That little nothing. She's so ugly. Ugh!
Your loving
Miranda

Darling Bobby
You must be suffering agonies from not being able to make love to
me. I know I would be if my vagina had failed to open for your
beautiful cock. I'd be desperate. I'd probably kill myself. Please
don't think of doing anything like that. I know I can make you
feel like a man. A real man. Just imagine being big and hard
and filling me up and us both coming together. I admit I'm in my
sexiest underwear as I write this and I'm so hot. I'll have to use
my fingers on myself. I'm doing it now with one hand.
Oh, Bobby!
I love you.
Miranda XXXXXXXXXXXXXXXXXXXXXXXXXXXX

Bobby
I'm desperate. Please contact me. We could be so happy and instead
I'm so miserable. Well, I'll make you even more miserable if you
go on like this. I won't be responsible for what happens. I can't

41

bear to think of you with her. I hate her, hate, hate, hate. I wish
she was dead.
In sorrow
M

I read the emails through a few times and leaned back to consider what conclusions I could draw from them. A narcissistic personality clearly, combined with brittleness and insecurity. Bobby had told me that the real threats had come in the messages sent through the website. In these she was just warming up. What I couldn't decide was whether what she wrote was genuine or feigned. There was something formulaic about it, particularly the sexual come-on. It read a bit like an excerpt from the advertisements for phone sex. But perhaps that's the only note you can strike when in the throes of sexual hysteria. I wasn't sure.

I copied the emails into the file and updated the memory stick. Bobby had given me the name of the street and the number of the building, but not the number of the flat. Not surprising. It was late at night and he'd had a fair bit to drink. Also, presumably, he was in a confused mental state. When he said she wasn't there any longer he said it the way an ordinary citizen does. I wasn't an ordinary citizen and I was pretty sure I could find out something more. I took my mobile off the charger and made sure it was fully functioning.

Bondi again. How many times had my work taken me

there? The place seemed to have a magnetic attraction for problem people and for me. Maybe I was one of them. I surfed there as a teenager and perhaps that helps to impose a grip that won't let go. Over the years I've toyed with the idea of moving there. Feasible at one time, not so easy now with the prices and my new mortgage. Driving down Bondi Road, just the look of the water, grey though it was, revived memories of it when it was blue and the feeling of scudding along on a wave towards the white pavilion and the brown bodies on the sand.

I located the street and drove slowly along to the address Bobby had given me. The street was tree lined and pleasant with a mixture of houses and flats. There would probably be glimpses of the water from the upper levels. The building I was looking for was newish and smart. It had a low fence, trees and shrubs in the front, ten letterboxes at the gate and a winding pebblecrete path.

It was a set of serviced apartments, the kind that can be leased for long or short periods. Almost hidden underneath the stairs was a small concierge desk with a woman sitting bent over, staring at the screen of her mobile phone and with her fingers flying. She was in her twenties, blonde and good-looking. When she heard the door close behind me she looked up.

'Can I help you?'

I showed her my brand spanking new licence card in its leather folder and tried to look as young as the photograph.

'I hope so,' I said. I handed her Miranda's photograph. 'I'm looking for this woman. I believe she lived here recently.'

She put the mobile on the small desk in front of her and studied the picture. 'Is she in trouble?'

'Possibly.'

'Wouldn't surprise me.'

'You know her?'

'Wouldn't say that. She was here for a while. Very short term.'

'What apartment was she in? Do you know her name?'

She shook her head. 'Never learned it. Didn't want to. She was a stuck-up bitch. She was in twelve, one bedroom job.'

'There must be a record of her time here, rent paid and all that.'

She took a card from a drawer. 'Letting agents. They'd have that stuff. They're in Campbell Parade. The address is on the card.'

I took the card and thanked her.

'Are you really a private detective?'

I nodded.

She sighed. 'That must be exciting. Don't need a secretary, do you? This was the only job I could get although I've got a lot of skills. I sit here playing games on my phone.'

'Sorry. Maybe something better'll come along. Do you remember anything in particular about this woman, apart from not liking her?'

'Like what?'

'Friends.'

She snorted. 'Wouldn't call them friends. All blokes.'

'Do you mean what I think you mean?'

'Sure do.'

I thanked her again and left.

The guy in the estate agency was far less forthcoming. He was young, wore a dark suit and had gelled hair.

'I'm afraid I can't give you any information at all,' he said.

'I'm sure you can. For example, what's the rent of apartment twelve? No harm in telling me that, surely.'

'Two thousand two hundred dollars a month.'

'Is it occupied now? I might want to rent it.'

As urged by Megan, I'd invested in some new clothes and I was wearing a lightweight grey suit and a blue shirt. No tie, but the shirt was tucked in.

A pause, and then he said, 'It's empty.'

'Things are slow?'

He didn't reply. I thought about mentioning the purpose to which Miranda appeared to have put the apartment but decided not to because it might cost the young concierge her job.

'Look,' I said, 'I don't want to make things difficult for you but I've got a client with a very serious complaint against the woman who rented that place. He's an important person and he doesn't want to involve the police. That's why he's employing me. But if I don't make progress it'll bring the police in eventually. Give me her name and forwarding address and that's the last you'll hear of it.'

He wasn't happy. He looked across at the empty desk in the office as if hoping someone would materialise there. No such luck. He tapped on his keyboard.

'Mary Oberon.'

'Forwarding address?'

'Twenty-six Hood Street, Burwood.'

'I'm guessing she paid a substantial amount up front.'

He nodded.

'Phone?'

He read off a mobile number and I wrote it in my notebook. Second bit of paper in the case. 'You sighted the ID?'

'Not me, but somebody must have. That's all . . . please.'

I could have pressed him for bank details and other things but I took pity on him. Suspicious sceptic that I am, I had doubts that the information was genuine. Perhaps the name, if I was lucky, but false ID isn't hard to get.

I had a track of Springsteen's *Nebraska* playing when my mobile rang. Hank Bachelor had equipped me with a hands-free hookup and I kept driving instead of pulling over as I used to have to do.

'Hardy.'

'Cliff, it's Bobby. You were right. There's a white Commodore following me.'

'For how long?'

'I don't know. I just picked it up. But I'm pretty sure.'

'Where are you?'

'Strathfield.'

'How many in the car?'

'One, two—I'm not sure.'

'On the highway?'

'No, I was heading for the golf course. I wanted to take a look at it. I'm going to play there next . . . Jesus Christ!'

'What?'

'He's crowding me off the road. I have to stop. Shit, oh shit . . .'

I heard two sharp reports and then nothing except the buzz of an open connection.

'Bobby! Bobby!'

The buzz stopped.

I had no idea where the Strathfield golf course was, or how many ways there were to get to it. He said he'd been out to Parramatta, which gave me some indication, but apart from that I'd have to rely on the *Gregory's* and luck.

Put your makeup on, fix your hair up pretty
And meet me tonight in Atlantic City.

I cut Springsteen off and headed for Strathfield. When I reached the outskirts I stopped and checked for the golf course, then plotted a way to it as if I'd been coming from

Parramatta. That took me through a grid of suburban streets until I saw a cyclone fence at the end of a road that looked like the sort of thing golf clubs use to keep people out. The area looked pretty affluent and the houses had the appearance of places occupied by families with both parents working to make the mortgage. I drove down the road towards a wide stretch of parkland bordering the fence. I made the turn to follow the fence and saw a red car a couple of hundred metres away. It had pulled a short way off the road and was slewed slightly to the left. As I approached I could see a skid mark on the road. I pulled up behind the Alfa.

An arm was hanging loosely outside the driver's window. I sucked in a deep breath, got out and approached the car. A long scrape indicated where the Alfa had been swiped by another car. Bobby Forrest was slumped forward, anchored by his seatbelt. There were two dark holes a few centimtres from his right ear. Blood had clotted around them and seeped out and matted his fair hair.

I stood and looked at him for a minute or two before I called the police. One meeting and a phone call didn't amount to much of a contact. But he'd told me things he'd only told one other person—his father. Somehow that mattered. The older I get the younger the young seem, and Bobby Forrest had seemed very young. I felt a mixture of emotions—pity, anger, guilt—as I keyed in the numbers.

4

Over the next few hours I told the story four times—to the uniformed cops at the scene, to the detectives there, again at Strathfield police station and again at the central police complex at Surry Hills. That took us well into the afternoon. I was tired, hungry and strung out. I'd had too much dispenser coffee; the taste in my mouth was foul and my mood was worse. My hands were dirty. I'd been tested for gunfire residue and the tissues I'd been given to wipe the testing solution away hadn't done the job. They'd taken the SIM card from my phone.

Detective Inspector Sean Rockwell's mood wasn't much better than mine.

'How long have you been back in business, Hardy? A month?'

'Bit more.'

'And this happens.'

He consulted a sheaf of computer printout. As well as telling the police what had happened I'd given them the memory stick and they'd printed out the Forrest file. Nothing else I could've done. They'd have seized the computer in any case and I already had a conviction for withholding evidence. A private inquiry agent has no privilege of confidentiality, especially when no lawyer has been involved in the case contract. Rockwell's look of disgust snapped my fragile control.

'Do you know why this bloke came to me? I'll tell you. Because he was worried about a serious relationship he was in and, quite reasonably, he knew that if he went to you lot the story would leak out to the media within the hour and he'd be fucked. That's why. He wanted me to handle it . . . discreetly. It all went wrong and I'm sorry about it, but don't come all high and mighty with me. I've said all I'm going to say and stayed long enough. Charge me with something or let me go.'

'I'd love to,' Rockwell said, 'charge you, that is.'

'I bet you would, but you've got nothing on me. You know everything about it I know. His mobile'll confirm he rang me just before he was shot.'

'No sign of his mobile.'

I shrugged. 'The killer must have taken it.'

'Or you did.'

'Why would I do that?'

'Who knows what a loser like you would do? Anyway, we don't quite know everything. We don't know what you found out when you checked on this . . .' he looked down at some notes he'd made, 'Miranda's address.'

'Dead end, I told you. Short-term rental. She was on the game. Your blokes there must know about it, probably got freebies.'

He slammed his fist on the desk and some of the sheets of paper slipped to the floor. 'Piss off, Hardy. And stay right away from this fucking mess you've created.'

'Where's my car?'

'Impounded for further investigation.'

That meant they'd take it apart carefully and just stick it back together any old how or not touch it and just hang on to it to punish me.

'My house keys?'

'Collect them on your way out.'

I was escorted from the interview room to the front desk where I picked up my keys. They kept my SIM card and I was issued with a receipt for it and my car. As soon as I got outside I was bailed up by a clutch of reporters—cameras, microphones, tape recorders, the works.

'Mr Hardy, was Bobby Forrest on drugs?'

'Why did Bobby hire you?'

'Was it suicide?'

'No comment.'

I pushed through them and hailed a taxi. They persisted while I got in, still filming and firing questions. They'd be at my house for sure. I gave the driver Megan's address in Newtown and he had the sense not to say a word for the whole trip. Perhaps he was a central police station specialist.

Megan took one look at me and stood aside. She was holding Ben and he reached out to grab my hair. It was better than being asked questions.

'I need a drink,' I said. 'A big one.'

Megan had seen me stressed quite a few times before. She just nodded. 'You know where it is.'

I made a large scotch and ice and took a big pull on it before sitting down. Megan put Ben on the floor and he surprised me by tottering across to a shelf of toys and pulling some out.

'He's only ten months old.'

'Nearly eleven. He's early at everything. Be careful what you say. He understands a lot. What's happened, Cliff? You look a wreck.'

It was close to six o' clock and I asked her to turn on the television news. The death of Bobby Forrest and my encounter with the media was the lead item.

The body of actor Bobby Forrest, star of several television series and recently cast in the lead role for a major film, was found at Strathfield today. It is understood that the body was discovered by private investigator Cliff Hardy who, it is assumed, was working for Bobby Forrest. It is not known what Mr Hardy was employed to do or exactly how Bobby Forrest died except that a gunshot was involved. Speculation that Hardy was acting as a bodyguard has not been confirmed. He was interviewed by police for several hours this afternoon but would make no comment. Bobby Forrest . . .

The report went on to give more details about Bobby's career and included several clips from his television appearances. I worked on the drink and let it all wash over me. Megan turned the set off at the end of the item. Ben was building a tower of cardboard blocks. He had it up nearly as tall as himself and when he put the last one in place he gave a whoop and knocked it down.

'I hope you weren't his bodyguard,' Megan said.

'I wasn't.'

I sketched in some of the details while I helped Ben rebuild his tower a few times.

'The police don't really suspect you, do they?'

'No. But they've warned me off having anything more to do with it.'

'If I know you . . .'

'He gave me a solid retainer. I'm honour-bound to work it off.'

'Yeah, yeah. You can't afford to step too far out of line.'

'Never could.'

'And it never stopped you. Do you have any idea who killed him?'

'No. It was a nasty, tricky business, but I had no idea it was this serious. Have to think about it.'

We dropped the subject, picked it up again for a while when Hank came home. These days he's mainly doing electronic security work, and when I told him the police had taken my SIM card he looked worried.

'Means they've got all your contact details and data.'

I shrugged. 'No data to speak of, not at this stage, and I've nothing to hide, really. But does that mean I've lost all that stuff?'

'No, dummy. When I set up your phone I fixed it so your contacts would be stored in the phone itself. Let's have a look.'

I handed him the phone, he fiddled with it and nodded. 'Yep, all there. I'll put in a new SIM card and you're up and running.'

Ben went to bed. Megan made dinner. I cleaned up. I slept on the couch, soundly, with two solid scotches and half a big glass of white wine inside me. I distracted Ben for a while in the early morning while Megan got things done and then walked home. No media, but cigarette butts, a couple of crumpled tissues and the open lid of my letter box showed that they'd been there.

I reviewed what I had on the computer file and added the one thing I hadn't told the police—that I had a forwarding address and a name for 'Miranda' from the serviced apartments' concierge. If they followed up my interview with her they'd find that out, probably, but it might take them some time. I could see if there was anything to be learned at 26 Hood Street, Burwood, just to feel that I was still earning Bobby's money. And because I don't like being told what and what not to do. If I found out anything useful I'd probably tell the police. Not necessarily. A one-man, unpaid hunt for a murderer still held an attraction for me, at least theoretically.

Before shutting down the computer I tried again to mentally recreate the driver of the white Commodore. I'd told the police I'd only registered that it was a male—from the build, the set of the head on the shoulders. Now I pushed myself to see if there was more. I'd mostly seen him from the back, only fleetingly from the side when he jerked his head sideways as he jumped lanes. There was something. But what? I couldn't dredge it up. Something.

I showered, shaved and took my medications plus some of those I'd missed the day before. Not recommended, but medicos who lay out rules for you don't anticipate things like being hauled in by the cops. Ben had spilled ice cream on the suit trousers. I changed into drill trousers, a casual shirt and a leather jacket. I hadn't told Megan and Hank about Bobby's mobile being missing. That meant the killer knew about me. Might care, might not. But I felt better with my new Smith & Wesson .38 in my armpit.

I walked to the ATM in Glebe Point Road, drew out a few hundred dollars and caught a taxi to a car hire place in Leichhardt. I opted for a blue Holden Astra which looked like about a hundred thousand others. It had the hands-free mobile phone attachment and GPS. After consulting the manual and getting it all wrong a couple of times, I got it to function with a pleasant female Australian voice. I entered the Burwood address and resolved to follow the instructions even if I thought I knew a better way.

I didn't know much about Burwood. I had an impression there were sets of medical clinics in the main drag and I seemed to remember something about citizens protesting against plans to open a brothel. I had a vague recollection that the argument was the brothel was too close to a church and a school. Can't remember how it came out, but to my mind churchgoers should be able to resist temptation or try to redeem sinners, and no brothel owner I knew would ever admit a schoolchild. They might have employees dressed up as schoolchildren but that was between them and their clients.

The GPS instructions got me to Hood Street more efficiently than I could have done. Spent almost no time on Parramatta Road. The house was a big Federation job on a corner. Biggish block, neat front garden, car access at the side. The area was quiet with an almost oppressive feeling of respectability. I parked outside, opened the low gate and walked up a tiled path to the front porch. The porch was tiled as well and the house carried a brass plate with the name 'Sherwood' in elaborate script. Some kind of joke. The brass was polished to a high shine.

I rang the bell. Footsteps sounded on a wooden floor. I had my licence and the photo of Mary Oberon or 'Miranda' at the ready. The woman who opened the door checked that the screen door was locked before she looked at me.

'Yes?' she said.

She was middle-aged, dumpy, overdressed in expensive matronly clothes. I showed her the licence and told her I wanted information about the woman in the photograph. Her heavily ringed hand flew up to her mouth.

'Oh my God, is she dead?'

'Why would you think that?'

She shook her head. 'Please go away, I don't want to have anything more to do with her.'

'This is important. I gather she's not here. Can I come in and talk to you?'

'No. Go away.'

'This could be a police matter.'

Her hand against the screen door trembled and I took a punt.

'Or a tax matter.'

The trembling increased.

'I don't want to make trouble for you,' I said. 'I don't even need to know your name. I just need to know everything you can tell me about this woman.'

'You'd better come in.'

She unlocked the screen door and I followed her a few steps inside and then into the front room on the right. It was a big room, overfurnished, with a bay window. The shelf in the bay window was covered with knick-knacks.

'Do you want to sit down?' she said.

The big armchairs would have swallowed me. 'No thanks.'

She subsided into one of the chairs. 'I should never have taken her in. She was unsuitable.'

'What name did she give you?'

'Mary Oberon.'

'Do you know what job she had?'

'She didn't seem to have one. She slept most of the day. She didn't have breakfast or lunch as far as I could see. I asked her if she was dieting and she laughed. She went out for a little while in the evening, to get something to eat, I suppose. Then she stayed in her room playing dreadful music.'

'She was hiding?'

'Hiding? I don't know. She seemed nice at first but she wasn't. Wouldn't give me the time of day.'

'How long was she here?'

'A few weeks.'

'She paid her rent?'

Tricky territory for her. There were, at a guess, four or five bedrooms in the house. She could be raking it in. She nodded.

'Why did you think she might be dead?'

She began to twist one of the rings on her finger. The sort of fidgeting that usually precedes a lie. My guess was that she'd poked into Mary Oberon's belongings or overheard something and didn't want to admit it. She looked around the room and didn't speak.

I shrugged. 'Okay, well I'll have to take it further, Mrs . . . ?'

'She was terrified.'

'Of what?'

'A man.'

I sat on the arm of one of the chairs. That perched me well above her in a dominant position. No great achievement; she was a guilty, frightened woman and I wasn't proud of pressuring her.

'Tell me,' I said.

She said Mary Oberon had paid a month's rent in advance. I'd have been willing to bet she'd extracted an extra month as a bond of sorts but I didn't interrupt her. She'd left before the month was up taking everything with her, which wasn't much to start with—clothes, toiletries, a computer, a mobile phone, an mp3 player which the woman called an earplug thing. I asked how she knew the music was terrible if Mary Oberon had listened through earplugs. She said she heard it sometimes when Mary played it without the earplugs just to annoy her. She left after being threatened by the only visitor she ever had—a bearded man driving a white car.

'Threatened how?' I said.

'They had arguments the couple of times he called. He woke her up in the morning and I could hear their voices raised.'

I bet you could hear them, I thought. *Raised or not.*

'Then one afternoon he came and they went outside. It looked as though he was trying to make her get into his car. I was watching from the side window. She wouldn't go. He got into the car and he tried to run her over. He drove the car over the gutter and up onto the nature strip and she had to jump out of the way. She fell over and he drove off. You can still see the marks the car wheels made on the grass.'

'Did you go out to her?'

'No, I was too frightened. I thought he might come back.'

And you didn't want to get involved. 'What happened then?'

'She came in and I heard her crying in her room for a while. I went shopping and when I came back she was gone. No note. She took the key to the house and her room. I had to change the lock on the front door and get . . . two more keys cut.'

And then some, I thought. I felt sure she knew more than she was telling me but had no idea how to tease it out other than by being direct. I stood and then sat down abruptly. She almost yelped in alarm.

'There's something you're not telling me. What is it? Quickly.'

'It's nothing.'

'Tell me.'

'Will you leave if I do?'

'Probably.'

'Wait here.'

I didn't. I followed her out of the room and down the passage to the kitchen. Her purse was sitting on a bench. She opened it, took out a banknote and handed it to me. It was a Fijian fifty-dollar note.

'I found it down behind the bureau in her room. Please take it and go.'

I put the note in my pocket and moved away. 'Why did you try to keep this from me? Don't tell me you thought she might come back for it.'

'Because I don't like you.'

'It's mutual.'

I left the house and went around the corner. There were two deep gouges in the grass on the nature strip about a metre in from the kerb. Impossible to tell whether it had been a serious attempt to run the woman down, but it was certainly enough to give anyone a hell of a fright. I looked up and saw the woman watching me from the house. The curtain twitched back closed when she saw me looking. I wondered if she'd reconsider her next tax return. Probably not, that kind of greed is ingrained.

Back in the car I looked again at the photo of Mary Oberon. Her skin appeared to be dark but not very dark, her eyes slanted slightly and she had a fine blade of a nose. A strong suggestion of Indian ancestry I hadn't noticed before. I started the engine and at that moment what had swum at the edge of my consciousness about the driver of the

Commodore came into clear focus. The man had a jutting chin and a beard.

On the drive back to the city I considered the information I'd picked up. An Indian prostitute being threatened by a man who looked likely to be the one who'd killed Bobby Forrest. Hard to make sense of, but it suggested a course of action if I was inclined to take it. Should I? I knew I wasn't directly responsible for Bobby's death. He wouldn't have wanted me to bodyguard him. I anticipated that he might be under surveillance and had warned him, but I hadn't thought he was in mortal danger. But that raised another concern. Had he put himself in that danger by hiring me? That possibility nagged at me all the way back to Pyrmont.

My mobile had been buzzing and chirping practically all day. I sat in my office, scrolled through and thought about deleting all the unfamiliar numbers and names. Most of them were bound to be media people, calling and texting, looking for dirt on Bobby Forrest, but you never can tell. I worked through them, deleting the media stuff, which left me with calls from Frank Parker and Megan and a text with the source blocked that read: *leave it alone. he had it coming.*

5

I rang Frank and assured him that I was okay and probably not facing any serious problems with the police. He offered to help in any way he could and I told him I'd keep that in mind.

'You're not going to follow this up, are you?'

'Only if it follows me.'

'Jesus, Cliff. Let it go.'

'Probably will.'

It was a constant theme with my friends—advising me to stick to the nuts and bolts of my business and not go involving myself in the labyrinth of people's problems. My ex-wife Cyn had said it was a psychological quirk that I should try to do something about.

'How?' I'd asked.

'See a psychiatrist.'

'I've seen too many Woody Allen movies to take them seriously.'

That started a fight, one of many. Cyn didn't find Woody funny.

Megan didn't join the 'leave it be' chorus, not explicitly, but she did want to know whether I'd need the couch again and I told her I wouldn't. Part of me wanted to let it go and just maybe I would have if it hadn't been for the text message. That made it personal and Bobby had paid for at least a few days' more work. I scribbled down the text message and looked at it. 'Had it coming' suggested something in the past rather than the trouble Bobby had brought to me, but I had no handle on that. Sophie Marjoram hadn't helped.

I left the office still undecided about what to do. I drove to Glebe and took a careful look along the street before pulling up at my house. Still no sign of the media pack. I got out of the car and was about to lock it with the remote control when I became aware of someone bearing down on me from across the road. He was big and moving fast.

'You bastard,' he shouted and swung his fist at me.

It's a good idea to be moving forward when you punch but only if it's a straight punch. Move forward and swing roundhouse and you're liable to lose your balance. That's what he did. The punch missed anyway because I swayed back away from it. I caught his fist as it moved past, twisted his arm and had him pinned against the car with one bent arm and the other flapping ineffectively. I leaned my weight against the bent arm. He swore and the fight went out of him.

'All right, all right. Let me go.'

He was big but a lot of the bulk was fat. He was breathing hard from just a few rushed steps and a poor attempt at a punch. I didn't think he could cause me much grief. I released him, stepped back and let him unwind himself. He grabbed at the car for support. He was red in the face and older than I'd expected. It was my day for putting the moves on unequal opponents.

He was wearing a dark suit over a black T-shirt; a pair of heavy sunglasses stuck out of the pocket where people used to wear display handkerchiefs. Maybe some still do. If he put them on he'd have something like the hoodlum look, but one who should leave the heavy work to younger men. He brushed himself down.

'Sorry,' he said.

'For what? That you didn't break my jaw? Who the hell are you?'

'You don't recognise me?'

'No.'

'Yeah, well, I've stacked on the kilos a bit. You don't look all that much different, Hardy. Greyer, few more wrinkles, but I knew you straight off. I'm Ray Frost—Bobby Forrest's father.'

We went into the house and I made coffee while he used the toilet.

'Crook prostate,' he said when he came out. 'Crook just about every other bloody thing but I'm still here.'

I poured coffee into two mugs. He refused milk and sugar.

'Got anything to give it a lift?'

I put heavy slugs of Hennessy brandy into both mugs and we went into the sitting room. He put his mug on the coffee table and felt in his jacket pocket.

'All right to smoke?'

I put a saucer on the table and drank some of the laced coffee while he coughed, got a cigarette lit and coughed some more.

'No point quitting,' he said. 'I could go any day and a few fags aren't going to make any difference.'

I nodded. He took a big slurp of coffee and a couple of lungs full of smoke and probably felt better, although he looked worse.

'You did me a very good turn twenty-odd years ago. Remember that?'

'I didn't remember the name but when Bobby told me about you I looked up the file. Yeah, it worked out okay for you, didn't it?'

'Right. When Bobby told me about his bloody problem I advised him to look you up. Charlie Bickford, the shyster— remember him?'

I nodded.

'Dead now. He always reckoned you were one of the few blokes in your game he could trust. He said you did the job and didn't play both ends against the middle like most of them.'

'I'm sorry for what happened. I didn't see it coming. It was a tricky business, all that online stuff, but it didn't seem . . .'

'I know. I know. Look, I'm sorry I took a swing at you. Not your fault. I just had to take it out on someone. My only kid. I'm going to miss him like hell. I have to do something about it.'

'The police are on it.'

'The cops.' He dismissed them with a wave of the hand that held the cigarette. Ash fell on the floor. 'Sorry. How many contract killings do they clear up?'

'You think it was a contract killing?'

He finished his coffee in a gulp. 'I can't get over the feeling that it was to do with me.'

I didn't tell him that I had something of the same reaction, but what he said put us on the same page. I took a good look at him while he worked his way through his cigarette. Apart from all the weight he would've been reasonably presentable but without Bobby's bone structure. That must have come from his mother. And Frost was dark. The gangsta clothes might have been an affectation or a necessary look. I went back to the kitchen and recharged our mugs. He had another cigarette going.

'What do you do that could get Bobby killed?'

'I run a business that provides men and machinery to construction companies. You wouldn't believe what goes on in the tendering process, the bribes, the deals, the fucking politics of it all. I step on toes all the time.'

'What kinds of toes?'

'Big ones. Bad ones.'

'Why the clothes? The Mafia image?'

'The people I deal with—union types, security guys— you've gotta look the part. I need your help, Hardy.'

'You've got a funny way of going about getting it.'

'I said I was sorry, for Christ's sake. What do you want me to do, kiss your boots?'

He was naturally aggressive, but so am I. 'Drink your coffee and make that your last cigarette. Passive smoking kills. Have you stayed out of trouble the last twenty-odd years? I seem to remember you were in a spot of bother once.'

He drained his mug and stubbed out the cigarette. 'I've sailed a bit close to the wind a few times, I suppose, but I've never had any charges laid since . . . what you're talking about. I was young and dopey back then.'

'Not that young. What d'you mean you need my help?'

'What do you bloody think? I want you to find out who killed my boy.'

'And then do what?'

He felt for his cigarettes, remembered and stopped. He shook his head. 'No, I'm not asking you to drop him in a hole. Let the law take over.'

He was hard to read. The aggression was real enough; it masked the grief, but that was real, too. Believing and trusting him was another matter. But how many of my clients had I fully believed and trusted? A majority, I thought, but not a big majority.

'Well?' he said. He wasn't pleading but he wasn't demanding either.

'Why me?'

'I remember that you were good. Discreet, didn't blab about what you were doing and you got it done. You're involved in this anyway. I've got blokes I could get . . . ask to do it, but they're too close to my business.'

'You don't trust them.'

'You could say that.'

'You reckon you've got candidates—people who might've wanted to hurt you this badly?'

'Yeah, a few. I don't know. It could still be connected to that fucking online dating shit. I wish he'd never . . .'

He broke off and looked at me, his eyes shrewd. 'You've got some ideas of your own, haven't you?'

I told him Bobby had paid me some money and that I'd followed up a couple of leads out of obligation. I said I had some more questions and some ideas about how to ask them.

'You mean *who* to ask them.'

'No, I mean *how* to find out who to ask.'

'You've lost me, but that's what I want to hear. Will you do it, Hardy? I'll pay whatever it takes.'

I wanted to do it and I had to do it. I had no other client and the publicity I'd got wasn't likely to bring people running. I felt the obligation to Bobby and an obligation to myself to follow up the leads I'd uncovered, and I've never liked leaving unfinished business.

I keep a few contracts in the house from the time when I worked at home. My contracts are about as bland and non-specific as the law allows. They simply state that the undersigned has agreed to commission my services as a private inquiry agent and agrees to the following terms and conditions. These relate to the schedule of fees, my responsibility to report findings and termination arrangements. Frost read it through very carefully. The space for the amount of the retainer was blank. He put a big, blunt, nicotine-stained finger on it and looked at me.

'Negotiable,' I said.

He nodded, took out his wallet and peeled off ten hundred-dollar notes.

'Give me your bank details,' he said. 'I'll transfer five grand today. Will that do?'

I filled the amount in on the form. He nodded, took a silver ballpoint pen from his breast pocket and signed both copies. I signed and gave him one copy. I wrote the bank account information on the back of one of my cards.

'I'll need names and any relevant information about the people you suspect,' I said.

He flicked the card before tucking it away with his Ray-Bans. 'I'll put it all in an email.'

'Just a few more things. Bobby's mother?'

'Died ten years ago. The usual, breast cancer. We were separated.'

'Have you met Bobby's girlfriend, Jane Devereaux?'

'Once. Nice girl.'

'That's all?'

'It was a very brief meeting. I've got to go. Arrangements to make when they release Bobby's body. Shit, have you got any kids?'

'One, a daughter.'

'Try not to outlive her.'

'Let me know the arrangements,' I said. 'I'd like to be there.'

'I will. Thanks, Hardy.'

We shook hands and I saw him out.

I phoned Frank Parker. He was in the city and we arranged to meet for a drink at a pub in The Rocks. I walked. I had two solid measures of brandy inside me on an empty stomach and the last thing I needed was a DUI problem. I enjoyed the walk through Walsh Bay and the sound and sight of the harbour always gives me a lift. The pub had a colonial theme but it's not overdone—no leg irons, no cat o' nine tails. I got there first and settled inside with a middy of light. In fact the theme was more nautical than correctional and I studied the paintings of tall ships as I waited.

Frank appeared carrying a stubbie. 'Got any convict ancestors, Cliff?'

'A couple, I believe.'

'Me, too. Cheers. Okay, exploit me.'

'Ray Frost, what do you know?'

Frank almost choked on his drink. 'Ray Frost—you're not in trouble with him, are you?'

'No, he's a client.'

Frank shook his head, took a drink and cleared his throat. 'I thought you'd have more sense.'

'Why?'

'He's a crook. He's also a ruthless bastard.'

'He said he hasn't been in trouble for years.'

'All that means is that he hasn't been caught. He's seen off a few people who got in his way. Not that they didn't deserve it.'

I remembered Frost's phrase, *I'm not asking you to drop him in a hole.* I said, 'He's Bobby Forrest's father. He wants me to help find out who killed his son.'

'Don't touch it.'

'He thinks it could be something to do with his business. Some kind of payback.'

'I wouldn't be a bit surprised. He's bad news, Cliff. He's a standover merchant. He puts pressure on people to accept his bids for jobs. Not only on the construction people, on the contractors and sub-contractors as well.'

'What kind of pressure?'

'Every bloody kind—financial, political, physical.'

'Wouldn't it be standard practice in that kind of game?'

'Frost took it to a new level. He's been up before a few Royal Commissions.'

'When?'

'The last one was only a couple of years ago.'

I drank some beer and wished I'd bought it full strength. 'I must've been overseas. When before that?'

'Back a bit. He's cunning and he's got some protection. What has he told you?'

'Not much. He says there's a few people who'd be capable of hurting him in that way. He's sending me the names.'

Frank finished his beer. 'I'm driving, that's all I can have. Don't take him on, mate. You'd be out of your depth. He'll be using you for sure. That's what he's good at.'

'He seemed genuine.'

'He would. Well, that's my advice. You'd be smart to take it.'

He patted me on the shoulder and left. I drank the rest of my beer and resented its thin taste. I bought a scotch and a sandwich. Graham Greene said the main function of food was to blot up alcohol. He had a point.

Frank's advice was usually good, but he shouldn't have said I'd be out of my depth. I was already wondering whether I was too old for the business and I didn't need my best friend to be expressing the same doubts. It made me determined to find out who killed Bobby Forrest and why.

On the walk back I thought about the lines of inquiry available to me. There was the matter of Mary Oberon and the bearded man in the white Commodore, and the payback possibility relating to Ray Frost. That seemed like the most promising order to tackle them in but there were two problems. The money said the last possibility was the one to work on, but was it the most likely? And who was to say that all three matters weren't related in some way?

It was dark when I got to Pyrmont. I was under the limit by then and could have driven but I decided to go up to the office and do some thinking. I turned on the computer and found I had three emails. Two offered me things I didn't want, the third was from Ray Frost. He was nothing if not succinct. All the message contained was three names: Charlie Long, Allied Trades Union; Ben Costello, MacMillan Bank; Philip Tyson, Sterling Security Inc. Tyson was the only one I'd heard of. He ran a service that provided armoured security vans with armed guards, bodyguards and nightwatchmen. He also provided training for these occupations and for staff for privately run prisons. He had a reputation for being a hands-on boss, possibly just the type to be in a conflict with Frost.

It would have helped to have some idea of what their disagreements with Frost involved, but he'd elected not to tell me. Anyway, I'd find that out when I probed into their affairs. I knew unionists, clients, at least, of bankers and I even knew of one of Tyson's former employees. There were things I could do to earn Frost's money.

The phone rang.

'Hardy.'

'Sean Rockwell. You can collect your car.'

That was a surprise. I'd been expecting a longer wait and an official letter. He told me it was in a police yard at Botany and that I could collect it there at 10 am the next day.

'Don't be late,' he added.

'How's that?'

'I'll see you there. We have things to talk about, like Mary Oberon and a house in Hood Street, Burwood.'

6

In the morning I took the hire car back to Leichhardt and caught a taxi to Botany. The police yard was a large bitumen expanse overlooking one of the container terminals. A chill wind was coming off the water and it looked and felt like just the right place for confiscated, neglected or abandoned vehicles. I showed ID and my receipt at the gate and walked across to where Rockwell was standing next to my Falcon. He tossed me the keys; I caught them, just, opened the car and looked inside. It was pretty much as I'd left it—that is, fairly clean.

'Let's get out of the wind,' Rockwell said.

I followed him across to a prefab office in one corner of the yard. We went in and a uniformed officer sitting at a desk stood up.

'Borrowing your office for a bit, constable,' Rockwell said. 'Go and have a chat to your mate.'

The officer nodded and went out. Rockwell pointed to a chair by the wall and sat on a corner of the desk. Dominant position.

'You must think we're stupid, Hardy. Or slack. Didn't you think we'd follow up on the address you gave us for the woman?'

'I thought you might, but I knew I'd do it quicker.'

'Despite being told to leave it alone?'

'Forrest gave me a retainer. I felt I owed him a day's work.'

'Bullshit. You could be facing an obstruction charge, like the one you served time for.'

'It was for withholding evidence.'

'That, too.'

I was puzzled. He was being too mild about it all. Why hadn't they just hauled me in to Surry Hills? The obvious answer was that they weren't making any progress, which was bad news in a high-profile case. It suggested they hadn't learned much at Hood Street. The obvious conclusion to draw was that the woman I'd spoken to wasn't there. They needed me.

'I want to know what you heard from the woman you spoke to at Hood Street—Mrs Thelma Harding.'

'Was that her name? She never said. Tell me what she told you and let's see how the stories match.'

Rockwell was an experienced cop, trained and practised at not displaying his feelings, but he looked embarrassed. 'She wasn't there. We found three Chinese students who'd

78

overstayed their visas. You scared the shit out of the one who was there when you called. He thought you were from Immigration. Maybe you said you were.'

'I didn't.'

'This bloke said you talked to Mrs Harding for a while and really put the wind up her. She packed a bag and pissed off, they don't know where. She told them to leave as soon as they could. Poor buggers didn't know what to do. Immigration's got them now.'

It's an old habit I'm unable to break—telling the police partial truths. They'd leaked the details of the Bobby Forrest murder to the media and would go on leaking. They suited themselves and my inclination was always to do the same. I told Rockwell about Mary Oberon being frightened of the bearded man in the white car. I told him about the attempt, real or not, to run her over. I didn't tell him about the fifty-dollar Fijian note.

'Is that it?' he said.

'That's it.'

'Not much.'

'No.'

'There must be thousands of guys with beards driving around in white cars.'

'Thousands.'

'Are you trying to be funny?'

I didn't answer. Rockwell had to decide and I wasn't going to make it any easier for him. He had to warn me off again or ask me to help. He wasn't dumb; he'd dealt with people like me before and suspected that I still hadn't told him everything I knew. He looked tired; he'd been working the case and getting nowhere. He eased off the desk.

'They tell me you're a mate of old Frank Parker.'

'Less of the old. He's only got a year or two on me.'

'He was a good copper. He gave a lecture once at the Academy. Impressed me.'

'He'll be glad to hear it.'

'You talk things over with him?'

'Sometimes.'

'I'm sure he'd advise you to cooperate with us.'

'Usually, yes.'

He couldn't quite bring himself to ask; that was as far as he'd go, but his meaning was clear.

He took a sheet of paper from his pocket and handed it to me. 'A few things you'd better fix on the Falcon if you don't want an unroadworthy certificate. We'll be in touch, Hardy. Make sure you're available for the inquest.'

I drove out of the yard and noticed that the petrol tank needle was on empty. I was pretty sure the tank had been at least a quarter full when I'd last looked. I spent an anxious ten minutes driving around looking for a service station and found one when the tank must have been close to bone dry. It looked like a spot of petty punishment and Rockwell's last comment about the car sounded more like a threat than a friendly gesture. After filling the tank I looked at the document I'd been given. The car had a cracked rear tail-light cover and a loose rear vision mirror on the passenger side. Hardly reasons to be taken off the road.

I spent the next two days at the computer, on the telephone and in pubs, offices and cafés, teasing out all the information I could about Frost's three names. It felt like old times and brought back to me why I enjoyed the work so much— the movement, the variety in the characters and situations and the way in which one piece of information led to another, or didn't. I felt alive.

Charlie Long of the Allied Trades Union didn't shape up as a likely candidate. He'd had run-ins with various people in the construction game, including Frost, but for some years he'd been keeping his nose clean. He was on track for an Upper House parliamentary seat and a likely ministry and was being scrupulously careful of his associates and his image.

Ben Costello, the merchant banker, had refused Frost a loan he'd badly needed a few years back and had financed one of Frost's competitors. Frost had struck back by buying a company Costello was in negotiation with on a financing deal that would have netted him a massive commission. Costello had a reputation as a vicious and vindictive operator who'd been mentioned in several ICAC inquiries although no action had ever been taken against him.

The shares in Costello's holding company had suddenly gone down, I was told by Tony Hunt, a blogger who specialised in inside information on the big players. That information cost Ray Frost some of his money.

'Why?' I asked.

'Silly question,' Tony said.

'Doesn't there have to be a reason?'

'Not really. The whole thing is a pack of cards house built on sand, to mix metaphors. A fantasy. That's what makes it so enjoyable to watch.'

'Could it be that ICAC is closing in on him?'

'You're no fun, Hardy. I like to think of it all as beyond reason and rationality.'

'That's not what you say when it comes down to paying you for information.'

'Sad, but true. You want me to find out what's scaring the market about Ben? It'll cost you.'

'Do it. Please.'

It sounded promising but it fizzled.

'Sorry,' Tony said when he rang back two days later.

'About what?'

'That I couldn't bleed you for more money. The cat's out of the bag.'

'I don't like paying for metaphors.'

'Like I said, you're no fun. Ben's got leukemia and is on

the way out. It was supposed to be a secret while he shifted the money around but it leaked out. Would you mind telling me why you're interested, Hardy? Information is a two-way street, you know.'

I declined.

I met Dominic O'Grady at the Botte D'oro restaurant in Leichhardt. O'Grady was a former private inquiry agent who'd turned to journalism. He'd worked for Sterling Security Inc and now wrote for the online investigative newsletter *The Sentinel*, run by my old friend Harry Tickener. O'Grady was a gourmand who'd undoubtedly order a massive and expensive lunch. I put in a long workout session at the gym in preparation for the meal and the wine that were bound to tempt me.

O'Grady was there before me, sitting massively in his chair by the window. He'd taken his jacket off and rolled up his sleeves, preparing for some serious eating. His belly kept him back from the table a fair way, but he was a big man with long arms. He was working his way through a bowl of olives and one of nuts. There was a bottle of white wine in the ice bucket and his glass was half full. The table napkin was tucked into his shirt below the first button and spread down towards, but not quite reaching, his gut. He looked up from the menu he was studying with the intensity of a stamp collector inspecting a penny black.

'Hardy, you bastard,' he rumbled. 'Good to see you. You did say you were paying, didn't you?'

'Gidday, Dom. My client is.'

We shook hands and I sat. He poured me a glass. I almost winced when I saw the bottle—French, of course.

'Ah, they were the days. Expense account lunches, padded out to buggery.'

'You don't look as though you're wasting away.'

He patted his stomach affectionately.

'Now, why I wanted to see you—'

'No, no, you philistine. First things first.' He smiled at the waitress who approached with another menu. She was dark and attractive, spike heels, tight skirt, lacy top. O'Grady emptied his glass. The waitress filled it and the bottle was empty.

'Antipasto, large,' O'Grady said. 'I think then the sword-fish. I'll cogitate on the dessert.'

'Chips and salad or vegetables, Dominic?'

'The former and another bottle of course. Hardy?'

'Swordfish good here, is it?'

'Everything is good, but the swordfish is superb.'

I ordered the swordfish with vegetables. The wine was cold, dry and fresh tasting—about as much appraisal as I can give the stuff.

'I understood Bobby Forrest was your client, but I hardly think he's paying for our lunch.'

'Another client.'

'Just back in business and two well-heeled clients already. I'd offer congratulations, but . . . Ah. Here we are.'

The waitress put a large platter of antipasto on the table in front of O'Grady. She showed him the wine bottle and opened it expertly on his nod. She produced a fresh glass; he tasted the wine and nodded again. He scooped up the few remaining nuts and olives and ate them before using a small fork to spear pieces of meat and cheese which he gobbled. He dived in again.

'Won't you spoil your appetite?'

'Age shall not weary it nor the years condemn. Just let me savour this for a few minutes before getting down to the no doubt distasteful business you have in mind. Do you want to share?'

I shook my head.

'Good.'

'Can we get started?'

'Always in a hurry, that's you, Hardy. Wait until I've had my first bite of fish. Have some more of this fine wine. Relax a little.'

With someone like O'Grady there's nothing else to do. It was late in the week, a popular time for lunching, and the restaurant was filling up. We were at a table for two with no other table really close. Ideal for a private talk. O'Grady was an old hand. I drank some wine and ate some bread. The fish came.

'Cracked pepper, Mr Hardy?'

I looked at her in surprise. I hadn't been in the place for years and had never seen her before. O'Grady chuckled.

'Fame, Cliff, fame. She saw you on television. It's the only thing that matters these days, unfortunately.'

I accepted cracked pepper and ate fish. It was good. O'Grady took some time with the dressing on his salad. He started on his fish.

'Phil Tyson,' I said. 'What can you tell me about him?'

'Nothing good. A thug. You know he sacked me.'

I nodded. 'But I want you to be objective.'

'Hard to be objective about Phil.' He ate a couple of large mouthfuls of the fish followed by a considerable number of chips and some salad in rapid succession. He chewed slowly and bowed his head reverently. 'Beautiful food, don't you agree?'

'It's fine. Thuggish how?'

'In every way—the people he hires, the pressure he exerts, especially on his clients.'

I stopped eating. 'On his clients?'

'I assume you're working for one of them. Not surprising. You should never tell your secrets to Phil. He'll handle your problem all right, but then he owns you and you have to dance to his tune.'

'Blackmail?'

'You could say that.'

'Do you happen to know whether he did any work for a bloke named Ray Frost?'

O'Grady ate and drank in his measured, appreciative way. He dabbed at his mouth with the napkin. 'I believe he did, yes.'

'Do you know what it was?'

He poured more wine and inspected the level in the bottle. 'Another, d'you think?'

'No. Tyson and Frost?'

'Sounds like a comedy team but I doubt there was anything funny about it. I don't know the details; it was after my time, but I imagine Phil straightened out Frost's problem in his usual direct manner and then extracted his pound of flesh.'

He compiled a forkful of food. 'Poor choice of words.'

'Direct manner?'

'Phil has a phalanx of heavies and they run about in a fleet of cars. I once saw the entire executive fleet turn up at the one place at the same time. Very intimidating. You're not eating.'

The fish was succulent and the vegetables were crisp but I was losing interest in the food. Something about O'Grady's rapid consumption and absolute enjoyment put me off. I toyed with what was on my plate for a while before putting my knife and fork down and taking a decent swig of wine.

'Disgusting,' O'Grady said. 'Sip it, man, sip it.'

'Why did you leave Sterling Security, Dom?'

'I blew the whistle on Tyson in 2003. I've got a flexible conscience but enough was enough. I thought everyone knew that. You disappoint me.'

I'd been in a fugue state for some time after my partner Lily Truscott had been killed, and then I'd gone overseas for a year or so. I'd missed a lot.

'And were there reprisals?'

'Oh, yes. Physical at first, now more or less just harassment. Unsettling. Tiresome.'

His plate was clean and he poured the last of the wine into his own glass.

'Doesn't put you off your food.'

'It did for a time, I can assure you. But it's an ill wind. I've got a comfortable spot now with Harry's rag. Will there be anything for me in this matter you're pursuing?'

'Absolutely not.'

'Thought so. Oh well, better make the most of this. Now I wonder what's best for dessert.'

I thought over what he'd told me as a way of fixing the information in my memory—*thug . . . heavies . . . pound of flesh . . . pressure . . . fleet of cars . . .*

'How many cars in the executive fleet?'

'Six.'

'What kind of cars, Dom?'

'White Commodores. Phil never uses anything else. Crème caramel, I think.'

7

Sterling Security Inc's website listed six senior associates: five men and one woman. No photographs. I thought it unlikely a woman would drive around disguised as a bearded man. I faced the prospect of getting a look at the five men to see if one was bearded. Not a strong line of investigation, beards come and go, but it was the best I could come up with.

I was back in the office. Frost's money had been deposited so that the balance in my account that took a heavy hit from the cost of the restaurant lunch was nicely topped up. I wrote down the five names and did the routine checks to find out more about them, particularly their addresses. No luck with the telephone directory; they were just the kind to have silent landline numbers if they had landlines at all. Mobile phone types for sure. But there are other ways. I'd lost my valuable RTA contact, which isn't much use for checking on people driving leased company cars anyway, but I still had one in a big credit checking outfit. The information was costly but reliable.

A phone call got me addresses for three of the names: Arthur Pollock, Blacktown; Stephen Charles, Randwick; and Louis Salter, Clovelly. Anton Beaumont and Ralph Cochrane were proving more elusive. But persistence paid off. Beaumont turned up in a newspaper report on a traffic accident in which he was involved and his address was given as Alexandria. He'd been taken to the Royal Prince Alfred Hospital for observation. I was pretty sure Hank could be persuaded to hack into the hospital records.

They say that there's nowhere to hide these days, but Ralph Cochrane was doing a pretty good job of it. He didn't appear on any of the databases I had access to and some discreet inquiries among people I thought might know yielded nothing. I could give him some thought. The procedure was going to mean a lot of driving around and trying not to be seen by people who presumably were good at not being snooped on.

There are people who do the easy stuff first. I understand the impulse but I'm the reverse. Get the hard stuff out of the way first. I'd always been like that—at school, in the army and in the profession I'd followed for so long. In the army it passed for keenness and efficiency. My reports spoke of 'diligence' and 'initiative'. It wasn't really, it was more a matter of doing the hard stuff while my energy level was high. I was easily bored and could get sloppy when I lost interest. As a detective the habit sometimes had benefits and sometimes not. Sometimes hard turned out to be easy and hard. You could never tell.

I wasn't sleeping well. A matter of loneliness and a feeling that I wasn't accomplishing as much as I should. So I was happy about making an early start. They say everyone is working longer hours these days and I assumed it applied to people in the security business, especially senior people if they wanted to stay senior. And why not me as well? I drove to Blacktown, setting off at 5 am, picking up the Great Western Highway at Five Dock and cruising through light traffic to arrive at the address a bit before 6 am.

Pollock's place was on the fringes in a street that featured large houses on big blocks with lightly timbered scrubland not far away. It was a short street and every house had a driveway but there were three cars in some places that looked to have two-car garages and a couple had a car in the driveway and another out on the street. Kids still living at home. One extra car wouldn't stand out too much. I parked on the opposite side of the street and about fifty metres away so that I'd get a clear view of Pollock as he backed out and swung around to face me before driving off.

The house was a two-storey job with white pillars, liver-coloured bricks and no eaves. Freezing in winter and stinking hot in summer, but presumably air-conditioned with a heavy carbon footprint. At 6.30 a roller door slid up and a white Commodore backed out. The driver obliged me by stopping before he reached the street, getting out and collecting the newspaper from the cylindrical holder beside the letterbox. He was small to medium sized with fair, thinning hair. No jutting jaw, no beard. He tossed the paper onto the passenger seat, got in and drove off without looking at me.

One down and four to go. I drove into the Blacktown CBD, found an early opening café and treated myself to a decent breakfast. I washed down my morning heart medications with some very passable coffee. Blacktown woke up around me. It appeared to be a busy, bustling kind of place with something of the feel of a country town as well as the big city.

The weekend interrupted the work. People follow different schedules, sleep in, go away and, anyway, a stakeout can look obvious. Monday was the day of Bobby Forrest's funeral. As Frost had anticipated, it was a big event attended by a lot of people from the entertainment industry, friends and the media. The ceremony was secular, at the Rookwood chapel. I'd been there too many times over the years and too recently.

The modern style is to 'celebrate the life' rather than 'lament the passing', but it's hard to do with someone so young. Frost did his best. He was impressive in his dark clothes.

'My son Robert was the best thing in my life. He's

gone but all my memories of him are good. He never once disappointed me or let me down and I tried not to ever let him down. That's what I mean by him being the best thing. He made me better than I really am and I'm grateful to him for that. I'll always be grateful for that.'

Pretty good. He echoed the words Bobby had used in explaining his relationship with Jane Devereaux. I suppose Bobby had said the same to him and he'd picked up on it. It was appropriate, and I thought Jane Devereaux would probably appreciate it.

A few others, including Sophie Marjoram and people from the entertainment business, spoke briefly. Bobby had been an organ donor and what was left of him was cremated. Among those attending there was a clutch of young people— goths and emos and the like—who stood apart. At one point I thought I could sense someone looking at me. I glanced at the young group and saw a woman in semi-goth clothes fixing me with a malevolent stare.

There was a wake, which they called a wrap party, at a restaurant in Surry Hills. I stayed long enough for a drink and to recognise a couple of the stars and semi-stars, some looking better than on screen and some not so good. I didn't get a chance to talk to Frost.

Over the next few days I went through the same surveillance procedure with Charles in Randwick and Salter in Clovelly with the same negative result. Neither man fitted the physical description of the one who'd followed Bobby and threatened Mary Oberon, though both were more impressive physically than Pollock. Hank was out of town on a job, which stymied me on Beaumont so I turned my attention to Ralph Cochrane. With no address available, the simplest way to get a look at him was to make an appointment to see him so that's what I did. It was a strategy I could use only once without raising questions and now seemed like the right time. Wouldn't hurt to get a close look at the Sterling set-up anyway.

Cochrane was described on the website as the 'Personnel and Training' manager. The obvious ploy was to inquire about the possibility of employment. The big security firms were swallowing the small ones continually and there was every reason for a senior personnel guy at Sterling to believe I was looking for a lifeline. I'd been head-hunted a few times in the past and had declined offers. That would have been known around the traps.

Sterling's HQ was in Rosebery, fairly close to the airport. Handy enough for the eastern suburbs dwellers, long drive from Blacktown. The building was an example of 1950s brutalism—a three-storey red cube set on a major road with no landscaping or trimmings—just a large bitumen parking area, a high cyclone fence and a manned security gate.

I drove up to the gate and told the guard my business. He consulted a sheet of paper on a clipboard, presented me with a visitor's pass on a lanyard and directed me to a parking slot.

I parked, slung the lanyard round my neck and followed white arrows painted on the blacktop to a set of double glass doors. The doors slid open, admitting me to a foyer. A woman sat behind a desk working at a computer. She was young and good-looking. Her long nails clattered on the keys.

She looked up. 'Mr Hardy?'

'Right,' I said, 'to see Ralph Cochrane.'

She pointed to an elevator. 'Second floor, room twelve.'

I thanked her and waited for the lift. The décor was functional—a few generic posters, a couple of citations for Sterling's creditable performance as an employer, a scale model of a projected new HQ. I rode the lift to the second floor and followed a corridor to room twelve. I could hear activity behind the closed doors—telephones ringing, machines humming. There were noticeboards along the wall bristling with pinned paper. Cochrane's name was on the door. I knocked.

'Come.'

I've never liked that response. Bad start and it got worse. There were three men in the room—one sitting behind a desk and two flanking it. As I entered one of the men moved behind me, closed the door and stayed there. The other standing man sat in the only other chair in the room apart from the one behind the desk. Not a friendly reception. The man sitting was Arthur Pollock of Blacktown, the smallish guy with the wispy hair. I didn't think I'd have too much trouble with him. I turned and looked at the man at the door. Much bigger, much younger. It's hard to judge the size of a man behind a desk but this one didn't look puny. He was in his thirties, dark and tanned. Maybe just back from his holidays, maybe a spray job. None of the men was bearded.

'I'm Ralph Cochrane, Hardy,' the man behind the desk said. He pronounced it 'Rafe'. 'This is Arthur Pollock and Louis Salter you know.'

'Do I?'

'Well, not exactly, but you saw him when you staked him out in Clovelly a few days ago. More to the point, he's seen you. Arthur seems to think there might have been a crappy blue Falcon like the one you drive outside his house, too.'

'Arthur's right,' I said. 'I didn't think he'd noticed.'

Pollock smiled. 'Subliminally,' he said.

'So you've shown a very great interest in us and we're wondering if we should be flattered or worried.'

'Flattered,' I said. 'I was considering trying to join your organisation and I was just checking a few of you senior people out before making an approach. That's why I made this appointment. I have to say I'm having second thoughts.'

I heard a movement behind me but I was too slow. A punch hit me hard in the kidneys, drove the wind out of me and buckled my knees. I had to grab at the desk to keep my feet. Salter looked pleased with his result as he should have. The punch was expert, placed in just the right spot and with just the right force. Deep bruise but no rupture, probably.

I fought for breath and almost gagged at the foul taste filling my mouth.

'Let the man sit down, Arthur,' Cochrane said. 'He needs the chair more than you do.'

Pollock stood and I collapsed into the chair and concentrated on sucking in air. It felt thin and insubstantial and as if it wasn't going to last.

'You've got a reputation as a tough guy, Hardy,' Salter said. 'I thought you'd be able to take it a bit better than that.'

My voice was a thin wheeze. 'We'll see how it goes next time, when we're face to face.'

'I'm off,' Pollock said. 'You can handle it from here. Let me know what he tells you.'

Cochrane nodded. Pollock took a step and I stuck out my foot. He stumbled and fell flat on his face. Pretty pathetic taking on the little guy but I had to do something. Salter stepped forward but Cochrane stopped him.

'Cool it, Louis. You okay, Arthur?'

Pollock got up, straightened his clothes and gave me a look meant to be venomous but it's hard to be venomous when your tie's crooked and your comb-over's been disturbed. He pushed past Salter and left the room.

'Let's start over again. Why're you so interested in us?'

I'd recovered my breath and straightened myself up in the chair. My kidneys had the ache that suggests blood in the urine. I'd been there before in my boxing days. My brain was working well enough though.

'I've got a question first,' I said. 'Your reaction is way over the top for spotting a little surveillance. What's got you so upset, Ralph?'

Cochrane and Salter exchanged glances and Cochrane nodded.

'You were seen having lunch with that fat aresehole O'Grady the other day,' Salter said. 'Someone passing by your table caught the name Sterling. You weren't discussing the fucking swordfish and O'Grady wouldn't be advising you to join this firm.'

'You're right there,' I said. 'He told me not to have anything to do with you but I decided to go ahead and see for myself. And I've seen all I want to see.'

'And what have you seen?' Cochrane said.

Something interesting that I'll keep to myself, I thought. I said, 'I've seen a couple of stupid guys worried about a fat man.'

'He's a journalist and he's never forgiven Phil for sacking him. You're snooping on his behalf.'

I tried to force a laugh but the action hurt too much. 'You're wrong. He says he never had it so good. He's enjoying what he does now. He reckons he owes Phil.'

They exchanged glances again.

'I suppose we could be wrong,' Cochrane said slowly.

I levered myself out of the chair suppressing a groan. 'Is that an apology?'

'Fuck you,' Salter said.

'You'll keep,' I said. 'I wonder if Phil knows how you're handling this?'

Salter looked worried; Cochrane didn't. He said, 'Phil's much too busy to worry about a nobody like you.'

Cochrane stood and put his hands on the desk. He leaned forward, so close I could smell his aftershave. 'You've wasted some of our valuable time, Hardy. You're a loser from way back and now you're scratching around trying to make a living. Well, don't scratch around here. Now piss off!'

He pressed a buzzer on his desk and an answering knock came on the door within seconds.

'Come,' I said.

Cochrane growled. The door opened and a woman stood there with an inquiring look on her face.

'Show Mr Hardy out,' Cochrane said.

I followed the woman down the corridor, into the lift and we went down to the foyer without a word being spoken. The glass doors slid open.

'Thank you,' I said.

She pointed to my chest. 'The pass, please.'

'I'll hang on to it as a keepsake.'

I glanced back at the building as I opened the car door. I thought I could see a figure standing at a window on the second floor about where room twelve would have been. I put the pass in my pocket and drove to the gate. The guard stopped me.

'Where's the pass?'

'I gave it to a woman inside.'

'No you didn't. She just called me.'

I nodded. 'Good security.'

I tossed him the pass and drove out.

I stopped at the first set of shops I came to and bought some painkillers. My back was aching and sending shooting pains up to my shoulders. I took three pills and sat on a bus stop seat drinking a takeaway coffee waiting for them to work. I stamped the image of Louis Salter on my brain—about my height and a bit heavier, maybe fifteen years younger. He had ginger hair and a long chin. The expertise of his punch suggested some kind of combat training, maybe military.

There was a reasonable chance of meeting up with him again. For one thing I still hadn't sighted Anton Beaumont, but there had been something distinctly conspiratorial about the behaviour of the three senior associates. I had no idea what it was about but they were overanxious about something. Salter had reacted oddly when I mentioned Phil Tyson. I wondered whether Phil knew how his minions handled apparently minor matters.

8

There was no blood in my urine and I bounced back pretty quickly from the kidney punch. My doctor, Ian Sangster, whistled when he saw the bruise.

'One of your best,' he said.

'Well placed,' I said. 'On the button. You can really deliver a whack there without fear of hurting your hand.'

'You'd know. Just watch yourself for a few days. There could be some collateral damage.'

'Like what?'

'Don't ask. I must say, apart from this you're in better shape than you were a while ago. Getting back to work's obviously good for you if you can just avoid the heavy stuff. How's your sex life?'

'On hold . . . wrong expression. In abeyance.'

He laughed. 'Use it or lose it.'

I thought about it as I walked down Glebe Point Road

to get a coffee and do some thinking. I'd underestimated the Sterling guys and knew I'd have to rethink my strategy to get a look at Anton Beaumont. Or maybe not. I'd rattled the other three; so perhaps it was time to keep on rattling.

I sat in the sun and ordered a long black and flicked through the paper. The minority government was still being cautious, the opposition was still being aggressive and the independents were still being as independent as they could. It wasn't very interesting but the opinion polls showed the voters were happy. Australians like a quiet life.

I rang Frost. I didn't have much to report but I wanted to ask him about the Sterling associates I'd met. Before I could do that he thanked me for going to the funeral.

'Sorry I didn't get a chance to talk to you,' he said. 'It was good of you to come.'

'It was a big turn-out,' I said. 'He was popular. I didn't see the girlfriend there—Jane Devereaux.'

'I asked her, left a message. I suppose she had her reasons.'

I asked him about the Sterling men.

'I know Cochrane. He's a tough prick. Don't know much about the others. Do you reckon Cochrane could have had a hand in it?'

'I don't know, but there's something going on there. The blokes I saw are up to something.'

'You mean a few of them could be involved in killing Bobby?'

'No, I've got the feeling it could be something in the future, but I suppose it could be connected.'

'Well, stick with it, Hardy. With you on the job at least I feel like I'm doing something.'

It wasn't a ringing endorsement but it was all I could expect. I finished the call and my mobile rang straight away. An unfamiliar female voice.

'Mr Hardy, this is Jane Devereaux, Robert Forrest's friend. I wonder if it'd be possible for me to see you.'

Robert? I thought. 'Yes, Ms Devereaux. How would you like to arrange it?'

'I've taken some leave. I'm quite free. I could come to your office. Would later this morning suit you?'

'That'd be fine. Do you know where my office is?'

'Yes, I have the card you gave Robert. That's how I know your mobile number.'

She was on time. She knocked confidently and walked in the same way. She was medium-size in height and build, looking taller in very high heels. She wore a dark skirt with an ice-blue silk blouse and carried a substantial briefcase. Her fair hair was curly and short. The photo I'd seen hadn't done her justice; she had fine-grained skin and though none of her features was striking taken separately, in combination her face became interesting and drew my attention. Her manner was assertive but her smile was shy. I stood and we shook hands.

'Thank you for seeing me, Mr Hardy.'

She had a slight countrified drawl. I asked her to sit down and watched as she lowered the briefcase to the floor. She sat straight; her skirt rode up exposing slightly heavy legs, flattered by the high heels. She wore light makeup, no jewellery other than small silver earrings.

'I'm sorry about Bobby,' I said. 'I liked him.'

'People did,' she said. 'I hesitated about coming to see you because I thought you might have given all those sordid details to the press.'

I shook my head but she went on before I could say anything.

'But I asked around and I was told it's not the sort of thing you'd do.'

'That's right. Do you mind my asking who told you that?'

'Harry Tickener. We're doing a book for him—a collection of pieces from his newsletter.'

'He's an old friend.'

'So I gathered. He encouraged me to come and see you.'

'What about?'

'I believe I know who killed Robert.'

I studied her for a second before replying. She seemed to be in command of herself, not showing signs of outward grief but carrying some kind of burden.

'Have you spoken to the police?'

She smiled. 'They interviewed me after Robert died. Not very thoroughly. I didn't tell them what I'm about to tell you. Did you read those tabloid articles about Robert and me? All that "plain Jane" and "brains before beauty" stuff?'

'No. I was aware of it though.'

'It was very hurtful and humiliating. I haven't got over Robert's death. I'm trying to, but it's hard. And I haven't got over that humiliation. I couldn't go to the funeral. I've written a note to Robert's father. It has affected almost everything I've done since. I've been made a figure of fun. The police wouldn't take me seriously. And I have no proof.'

'You'd better tell me about it.'

She straightened her shoulders and made herself more comfortable in the chair. 'I'm not a sexually attractive woman at first glance. I know that. My mother told me so. But I am very highly sexed and I've never had any trouble attracting men. I'm also highly disciplined and I knew an MA would help me get the kind of job I wanted in publishing. So I kept everything under wraps while I worked for the degree. It took a while to get the job and in that time I went a bit wild. I screwed around—men, women, youngish and oldish.'

I nodded.

'This is about two years ago. I've only had the job a little over a year. In that wild time I met a man and we had a very hot affair. A crazy affair. He was married. I broke it off when I got the job. I didn't need the distraction and there was no future in it anyway. He wouldn't let go. Maybe he tried; he went away for a while but he came back. I met Robert only a month or so ago and—'

'Sorry to interrupt, but if you say you can attract men easily why did you do this online thing?'

'It was in reaction to what I'm about to tell you. I decided to be more careful about men. When this man I'm talking about found out about Robert he threatened to kill him.'

'Threatened how?'

'Letters.'

'Have you still got them?'

'No, he broke into my flat and stole them.'

'You didn't tell . . . Robert about this?'

She frowned, which made her look older. I guessed she was a couple of years older than Bobby.

'It's ironic, isn't it?' she said. 'Robert kept his stalker from me, I suppose because he was afraid he'd lose me, and I did the same. I was very, very deeply in love with him. I wanted to keep him so badly. I wanted it more than anything I . . .'

She broke down at that point. Her voice fell away to a whisper and she sobbed quietly with her hands covering her face. She had slim, elegant hands. I took some tissues from a box on the desk, got up, took her hands away gently and gave her the tissues. She dabbed at her eyes and blew her nose. It was more ironic than she knew. They'd both been keeping the threats directed at the other to themselves.

'Thank you. I'm sorry. I'm usually not . . .'

'It's all right. When you're ready I've got a question for you.'

She nodded, drew in a breath and made a fist around the tissues. 'I'll answer if I can.'

'What kind of car does this man drive?'

She looked disappointed. 'Car? I don't know, something very expensive. Why?'

'I think the person who killed Bobby was driving a white Commodore sedan.'

Her heavily lidded eyes opened wide. 'Oh no, he didn't mean he'd do it himself. He meant he'd have it done.'

9

I don't think my jaw dropped, but I stared at her.

'Who are we talking about?'

'Michael Tennyson.'

'You mean "*Media*" Michael Tennyson?'

'Yes.'

Michael Tennyson was a merchant banker. He was big in conservative politics, big in the media, big in sports promotion and arts patronage. He was a flamboyant publicity-seeker who'd made all the right moves before the GFC and had escaped unscathed. There were rumours of criminal associations but there always are with high-profile types like Tennyson.

Jane explained that she'd worked as a freelance editor for several publishers and magazines before landing her present job. Tennyson was a part-owner of one of the publishers and they'd met at a gathering to launch a book Jane had helped to edit.

'It was a gala affair,' she said, 'as everything Michael had to do with tended to be. All the glitterati were there. You wouldn't think Michael would take any notice of me, but he did.'

Her face became animated as she spoke, perhaps recalling the heady days, perhaps from anger at what had happened. Her colour heightened and her eyes took on a strange intensity.

'I can see why he would,' I said.

'Can you? Well, he did and he came on very strong. There were letters and flowers and phone calls and meetings and gifts. And sex. Lots of sex. As I said, I got tired of it and didn't need it once I was working at something I loved, but Michael didn't. He went on a business trip to the States. He said it was to get over me after I'd told him I wanted the affair to stop. I don't think it was, not really. Overseas trips are just part of his normal agenda. He'd lie about anything to get what he wanted.'

'You said he broke into your flat.'

'I'm sorry, I was speaking loosely. I meant he had someone do it. Just as . . .'

'It's a very hard thing to prove. Do you have any kind of evidence?'

She was composed again now, with her intelligence rather than emotion showing. 'There's a man who works for him. Michael told me he'd killed people before.'

'And what's his name?'

'Alexander Mountjoy. I think he's a very frightening individual.'

The name didn't mean anything to me. 'What does he look like?'

'Big, bulky.'

'With a beard?'

She touched her face. 'Stubble. Michael used to boast about his criminal connections. I found it exciting. Briefly.'

Jane Devereaux put the crumpled tissues on the desk.

'You look sceptical, Mr Hardy. I'm no femme fatale, I realise that. Michael Tennyson's an attractive man in his way. He could have the pick of attractive women. He has a glamorous wife, of course. I just thought . . . Robert spoke so highly of you on our last night. Perhaps I'm wasting my time. You think I'm a fantasist.'

'No, it's not that. Not at all. I'm trying to understand something else. I hope I'm not offending you, but you seem to be an extremely intelligent and well-qualified woman, and Bobby Forrest . . .'

She smiled. 'You thought he was dumb?'

'No . . . limited, perhaps, in comparison.'

'Yes, I see. You have to understand that Robert was beautiful from the day he was born. Really beautiful, not just in the way that people say babies are beautiful. And he had an array of talents. He's . . . he was naturally athletic, musical and charming. He told me he'd never had a day's illness in his life. Not even a cold. I believed him. He never had to try very hard to be good at things and at the things that didn't interest him he got by, easily.'

She spoke with a firm conviction that was compelling. The attractive animation had resumed.

'He was very quick-minded. And he found in me something that mattered more than great legs and big tits, if you can believe that.'

'Yes,' I said. 'And you really believe Tennyson would have him killed because he'd been trumped by him?'

'Good expression. Yes, trumped by a dumb actor. All his money, all his power and influence. Trumped. He's a wild man under the suits, behind the designer glasses. He does wild, dangerous things and pays to cover them up.'

'Has he continued to . . . pursue you?'

'Yes, subtly.'

'What does that mean?'

She opened the briefcase and took out a slim box about ten centimetres long and three or four wide and deep. She leaned forward, put it on the desk and opened it. Inside, nestling in blue velvet, was a small, glittering object on a gold chain.

'What is it?' I said.

'It's a Fabergé egg.'

I'd read about them in books but I had no clear idea of what they were or what they looked like. 'I thought they'd be bigger.'

'Some are. This is one of the very traditional kind, to be given as a gift at Easter and worn around the neck.'

'Is it genuine?'

'I think so.'

'What's it worth?'

'Thousands. It can only have come from him. It's his way of saying he still wants . . . no, demands me.'

'What are you going to do with it?'

'Send it back, of course. Then there'll be something else. He won't stop. I remember him telling me how he went after a small business he was interested in. He persisted and persisted until he got it, even though he destroyed a few people along the way.'

'I'm surprised you had anything to do with him.'

'So am I, looking back. But I wasn't myself and I was flattered.'

I was trying to think what use I could be in the situation. 'Are you afraid of him, Jane?'

'Not physically, he wouldn't harm me, but I'm sure he could bring pressure to bear on the company I work for. He could cause me to lose my job and that's all I have to live for right now. I feel very vulnerable and I'm not sure I can cope with another loss.'

'Ray Frost, Bobby's father, thinks business difficulties of his might have caused Bobby's death. He feels responsible . . .'

'I understand. That's part of my distress, too.'

'. . . and he's hired me to look into it—see if he's right.'

'I can't afford to hire you. I just hoped you'd be interested enough to look into what I've told you. See if there's any way to sheet it home to Michael Tennyson. I know it's a lot to ask.'

I thought about it while she closed the box and put it back in her briefcase. She smoothed her skirt down with those fine hands and looked out through the window on the left side. It was the first time in a long while I'd had an office window clean enough to look out of. From the expression on her face she wasn't seeing the city skyline; she was looking at something shrouded and much further away—her future.

'In a way it isn't that much to ask,' I said. 'I've got several lines of inquiry to follow and yours is just one more. It's all part of the same thing. What happens if I find Tennyson wasn't involved?'

She shrugged. 'Then at least I won't feel responsible, and I'll deal with it more easily.'

I told her I'd do what I could. I made a note of the partial description of Alexander Mountjoy, some details of Tennyson's habits and interests and her own details. I advised her to upgrade the security of her flat and to get in touch with me if Tennyson approached her directly. She thanked me and left. It had all taken something over an hour. My back was stiff and sore from sitting and I was thirsty and hungry. I used the rail to help me get down the stairs and got an odd look from someone bounding up the stairs the way I used to bound. And would again, I told myself.

■ ■ ■

Pyrmont has sprouted cafés and coffee shops the way a gentrifying area will and I only had to walk half a block to find one. I was able to sit outside in the sun, sheltered from the wind by a heavy plastic sheet. I had a glass of wine and a Greek salad. I'd been in the place once before and was back because it was one of the few cafés that didn't overload the Greek salad with cucumber. Plenty of feta—the way I liked it.

As I'd told Jane, I had three lines of inquiry to follow— the Miranda/Mary Oberon stream, where it was a matter of trying to locate a Fijian-Indian prostitute and her white Commodore-driving assailant; there was Anton Beaumont from Sterling who drove a white Commodore and might be bearded; and there was Michael Tennyson and Alexander Mountjoy, neither of whom was bearded. Tennyson probably drove a BMW or some such, and what Mountjoy drove was anybody's guess. Tennyson probably wouldn't employ anyone close to him as a hit man, but he'd need a go-between.

The question was, which line to follow? I made the decision over a cup of coffee, breaking my rule about doing the hard stuff first because my back was sore. I decided to go the easy route and take a look at Beaumont. If he was clean-shaven and not jut-jawed behind the wheel of his Commodore, I could probably forget about Sterling. Let the boys play out whatever game they were up to.

I wasn't sure how to go about it but as things turned out part of it at least was made easy. I walked back towards the office and noticed a white Commodore parked rear-to-kerb across the street. It was a parking spot I coveted but rarely won. A man got out of the car, watched for traffic, crossed the street and came towards me. He was tall and solidly built and looked purposeful. I tensed. He came on and stuck out his hand.

'Cliff Hardy, I presume.'

He had an engaging smile and there were no visible weapons. I shook his hand.

'I'm Anton Beaumont from Sterling. I'd like to have a talk with you.'

We went up to the office and I tried not to make heavy weather of the stairs. Beaumont was at least ten years younger and fit. He didn't exactly bound up, but he could have. He wore a lightweight grey suit with the jacket unbuttoned over a blue shirt, no tie—no beard and no sign of one recently removed. I got him seated. Jane Devereaux's damp, crumpled tissues, slightly marked by her eye makeup, was still on the desk. I tossed it into the wastepaper basket.

'Upset female client?' he said.

'You're a detective. Why're you here, Mr Beaumont?'

'Anton, please.' He crossed his legs and got comfortable. 'One of my jobs at Sterling is to review the CCTV footage. You showed up. I recognised you from your . . . appearance on television a little while ago.'

I nodded.

'Mind telling me why you were there?'

I shook my head.

'Right, as expected and it doesn't matter. Why I'm here is because neither Cochrane, nor Salter nor Pollock mentioned your visit to me or to Phil. They don't know that I know you were there. I'm wondering why.'

'Perhaps they'll get around to it. They must've seen the footage. Maybe they're just waiting for you to ask.'

'Nope. They haven't seen the footage because they don't know the cameras have been installed.'

'Just you and Phil?'

'Just Phil and me.'

Good grammar, I thought. I said, 'Aren't you letting me in on some sneaky secrets, Anton?'

'For a reason. Those three bastards are plotting to take over Phil's company. I've got the job of stopping them. That's why I need to know why you were there. If you're involved with them I'm giving you the chance to tell me what you know and stay clear of the shit that's going to come down. Because they're finished and possibly going to gaol.'

So bang went one of my lines of inquiry. Without going into much detail I told Beaumont that my interest in Sterling had nothing to do with whatever the gang of three were plotting. He was equally reticent about what the plot involved and what measures he was going to take to stop them. We fenced for a while, batting cautious admissions back and forth, until he was satisfied.

We shook hands again.

'I hope you can resolve your client's problem,' he said, pointing at the wastepaper basket. 'I was on my own in the game for a while but I found it too tough. Needed a corporate structure.'

'Now you've found that tough.'

'In its way, yes. But more comfortable generally speaking.'

'By the way, how did you know where I'd be just now?'

He grinned. 'I've had someone following you since yesterday.'

'Didn't notice. I'm slipping.'

'She's very good.'

He left and I sat looking out the window Jane Devereaux had stared through. I was left with a problem. I was holding close to five thousand dollars of Ray Frost's money and I was just about certain his suspicions were unfounded. End of job.

I rang Frost's business number, spoke to his secretary and made an appointment to see him the following morning. I spent the rest of the day and the early part of the night on the computer researching Michael Tennyson. There was no way to read everything that came up on Google and if there's a way to determine what's important and what isn't, I didn't know it. I floundered around in the websites until I felt I was drowning in information.

I ended by printing out the best of the photographs and the basic biographical material. He was born in Sydney forty-two years ago. He was educated at private schools and Stanford

University. He inherited a pile of money and a thriving real estate business from his father and he diversified quickly and adventurously, never putting a foot wrong until he'd assembled the interlocking companies that went under the name of Tennyson Enterprises. He was married to Samantha nee Miles-Wilson and had a son aged nine and a daughter aged seven. His Sydney residence was in Bellevue Hill but he maintained apartments in several capital cities in Australia and overseas and a country property on the central coast of New South Wales.

Jane Devereaux had said he was attractive in his way and I could see what she meant. He was tall and, at a guess, gym-toned, with dark hair and perfect teeth. His eyes were a little too close together and his nose a bit sharp, giving him a foxy look. He played golf and tennis, fished and collected vintage cars. A list of his involvement in boards relating to money, sport and the arts would fill a foolscap page. He was a big donor to the conservative parties at state and federal level.

There was nothing about Alexander Mountjoy. The web, and especially Google's 'Images' site, picks up even very obscure people, but there wasn't a trace of him.

10

Frost ran his operation from a huge yard, dotted with sheds and several sizeable demountables, in Alexandria. Like the Sterling set-up it was surrounded by a high cyclone fence but some effort at beautification—a few shrubs, a strip of grass, a bench seat under a shade tree—had been made. Unlike the Sterling compound there was no security at the gate. I drove in and parked among a number of utes, trucks and pieces of earth-moving equipment.

The area was surrounded by light-poles connected by loops of heavy cable. At night the place could be lit up like a football field. A hand-painted sign stuck to one of the poles pointed me to the office in the biggest of the demountables. A few men in overalls bustled around the yard and I could hear the hum of generators. The office building was set on stumps a metre high. I went up a set of steps and in through the open door. The walls of the office were mostly covered with noticeboards holding pinned sheets of paper that fluttered in the draft from a fan.

There were two desks. Frost got up from behind one and came towards me with his hand out. We shook. His hand was hard and callused. Ray Frost might tread a fine line from a legal perspective as Inspector Rockwell had said, but at some time he'd done his share of the hard yakka.

I sat in the chair he indicated and he gave me a searching look.

'What's wrong with the back?'

'Kidney punch from one of the people at Sterling.'

'You get even?'

'Not yet.'

He grinned as he sat. His jacket was hung on his chair. His arms in the black T-shirt were tanned and meaty. 'You've been on the job, then?'

I told him how I'd come to focus on Sterling as the only likely candidate for what worried him and about the Sterling associates driving white Commodores. I outlined my encounter with them at their HQ. Then I told him about Anton Beaumont coming to see me, and what he'd said about the trouble at the senior level of the firm.

'Sounds as if Phil could have a fight on his hands. Good. I'm relieved that you don't think I brought it about. That helps a bit. But who killed him? I just don't understand it.'

'I haven't come anywhere near earning the money you've paid me.'

He waved it away. 'Doesn't matter. It's only fuckin' money. I'd give every cent to . . .'

'I want to keep working on it. I've spoken to Jane Devereaux. She's got a theory about what happened.

He opened a drawer in the desk and took out an envelope. He handled it as if it was something precious. 'She wrote to me. Explained why she wasn't at the funeral. I could see exactly what she meant. It's like they say—I could feel her pain. She can put things into words. Made me cry. It seems to me she would've been a terrific woman for Bobby. It's fuckin' unfair. They deserved better.'

I nodded. 'And there's something else I want to follow up.'

'You keep going, Hardy. Keep at it, and if you need more money just ask.'

'I don't want you to feel manipulated.'

'Nobody manipulates me, mate. Nobody.'

We shook hands again.

'And not just money,' he said. 'Any other kind of help you might need.'

I drove back to Pyrmont, still undecided about how to proceed. Jane Devereaux had been convincing, but tackling Michael Tennyson was a tall order. I'd have to do a lot of preliminary skirmishing to get a feel for the texture of his life and he obviously spent a lot of time in places I couldn't go. How to uncover his dark side, if he had one as Jane alleged?

I was in the office and about to phone Harry Tickener to see if he could help and also to get his take on Jane, when the phone rang.

'This is Cliff Hardy?' A light voice, accented, female.

'Yes.'

'I saw you on television. I have information about the death of Bobby Forrest.'

That's the trouble with television, you're exposed—it allows people to think they know you or can approach you. Just opening the conversation that way made me sceptical.

'What sort of information?'

'I am very frightened.'

'You should go to the police if you have information about a serious crime like that, and if you've been threatened.'

'I cannot go to the police.'

'Why not?'

'I am illegally in this country. Also I am a prostitute.'

That made me sit up. 'Things can be worked out for an illegal person who can help the authorities. And prostitution isn't a crime, I'm happy to say.'

She made a sound that could have been a laugh; hard to tell. 'Have you ever heard of honour killing, Mr Hardy?'

'I have.'

'If my family knew what I do I would be killed. I need money to get a very long way away from here and from them.'

I thought of Ray Frost's offer and wondered how much

he'd really be willing to cough up. 'I'd have to be sure that your information was valuable before I could offer you any money.'

'I know who killed him. I know the name.'

'You know the killer?'

'Not exactly. I know someone who does know him, that is how I know.'

It was getting woolly but there was something authentic-sounding in the voice. 'Perhaps we could meet and discuss it.'

'Yes, if you can bring some money.'

'I guess I could bring five thousand dollars.'

A sigh. *Disappointment?*

'That is not much.'

'There could be more if I'm convinced by what you say, and I could possibly help you with your problem.'

'Are you an honourable man, Mr Hardy?'

More honourable than a relative who'd kill you for being a prostitute, I thought. 'I hope I am.'

'Very well. I will meet you.'

'Where? And what's your name?'

She made that ambiguous sound again. 'Names. You could call me Miranda.'

'Are you Mary Oberon?'

'No, but I know her. Enough. Come to my place, 12A Little Seldon Street in Paddington. When can you come?'

'Give me three hours—say, four o'clock?'

'Yes.'

She hung up. I checked my bank balance. With Frost's deposit there was enough to draw out five grand and still continue to eat for a few days and meet the next mortgage payment. I wouldn't need three hours to draw the money and get to Paddington, but I'd need plenty of time to look the place over thoroughly and watch for comings and goings. The police had checked the .38 after I'd reported Bobby's death and returned it to me reluctantly. I took it with me but left it in the car—you don't walk into a bank carrying a gun.

No problem with the bank. You can draw out, deposit or transfer any amount up to ten thousand without questions being asked. But it left me with an uncomfortable feeling. Peanuts to some people, not to me. In hundreds, five grand is a fair-sized wad. Carrying it justified the pistol, even if going to meet an unnamed prostitute with multiple and complex problems didn't.

The mid-afternoon traffic was manageable. I was in Paddington with the better part of two hours to spare. I parked in a side street two blocks from Little Seldon and worked my way back. The only approach was along Oxford Street and then a few twists and turns down narrow streets. The area featured a mixture of big and medium-size houses, some terraces, some freestanding, mostly old, some new. There were several blocks of mid-size flats and the precinct was honeycombed with lanes.

Little Seldon Street was short and so narrow the footpaths

were only wide enough for one person. No trees. From a lane on the opposite side of the street I had a clear view of the house. It was an old workman's cottage, one of a pair, and couldn't have been more than three metres wide. At a guess, two up and two down. The balcony overhung the street. The door had been recently painted; the rest of it could have done with a new coat. It was a 'residents' only' parking set-up and most of the residents must have been off earning the mortgage repayments. Although all the houses were small they wouldn't have come cheap. The handful of cars in the street were unremarkable.

I scouted the block. A lane ran beside number 12A and down behind the houses. Hard place to keep watch on. At four o'clock I used the door knocker—no response. I tried again with the same result. A curtain fluttered at the open full-length glass door leading to the balcony. I knocked again, stepped out onto the street and called. Nothing.

I went down the lane to the back fence of 12A. It had a gate that was standing open. The door at the back of the house was also open. I unshipped the .38, crossed a tiny bricked courtyard and went into the house. The kitchen wasn't much more than a couple of cupboards and shelves and a sink. There was a toaster and a microwave. Then there was a small dining room and sitting room combined. The room was a shambles. The furniture, table, coffee table, TV and DVD set-up were almost miniature in size but they'd been smashed and the pieces distributed around the room. An aluminium rack that had held a set of pornographic magazines had been crushed underfoot and the magazines ripped to shreds. The DVDs were pornographic—huge-breasted women and men with giant penises on the covers. A lot of the discs were lying about, scratched and broken.

A photograph had been torn from its frame and torn to pieces so that it was impossible to tell what it had been. Someone had urinated on the pieces. Along with the smell of piss I could detect cigarette smoke, perfume and something else. I knew what it was.

The staircase was virtually a ladder—very narrow, very steep. I went up. The back room held a moveable clothes rack and a chest of drawers. Clothes were hanging out of the drawers and askew on the rack. A large suitcase lay open on the floor with clothes and shoes spilling from it.

She was in the front room on the queen-size bed that took up most of the space. She was naked under a white silk dressing gown, untied. Her skin was a deep brown and her tightly braided hair was black. The kind of scarf Muslim women wear was ripped and lying beside her. A dark stain spread from under her head across the white satin cover on the bed. Her head was turned and her dark eyes stared blindly at me.

part two

11

I couldn't afford to be the discoverer of a murdered person a second time in a matter of days. The police would tie me up in knots and the publicity would be disastrous. I gave myself five minutes to search the house for the identity of the dead woman. No sign of a handbag or a purse. I opened drawers using a tissue and probed using a ballpoint pen. No letters, no cards, no post-its, no mobile phone. Some of the clothes on the rack were professional—silk, satin and lace items—but the ones she'd been packing were practical.

I noticed something sticking a millimetre or so out of a pocket of the suitcase cover. I teased out a postcard-sized photograph. It showed three young women standing together in a linked, provocative pose wearing the appropriate clothing. One of them was the dead woman wearing a head scarf; one I didn't recognise and the other was Mary Oberon. I took the photograph.

I left the way I'd come in except that I stayed in the network of back lanes until I emerged a few blocks from Little Seldon Street. I walked to my car and sat there for a couple of minutes. The dead woman looked to be in her twenties; she was beautiful with a fine body. From her hair and features I guessed she was African. From her voice she was educated, and she'd sounded rational and intelligent. I felt her loss, not just because of the information I'd never get from her, but because she was much too young to die and she'd died a long way from home.

I drove until I found a public phone. I rang the police number and said where to find a dead woman.

'Sir, please give me your name and address.'

That 'Sir' at the start of the sentence. They pick it up from American television. It annoys me. I hung up.

Driving around with five thousand dollars in your pocket isn't the most comfortable feeling, particularly when you're heading where I was. The House of Ruby is a massage parlour and relaxation centre in Darlinghurst Road, Kings Cross. While being a hard-headed businesswoman, Ruby, the proprietor, is also something of a mother figure and mentor to Sydney sex workers. I'd done some work for her in the past, bodyguarding a couple of her employees and getting a threatening rival off her back. We're friends.

Marcia, her well-constructed and immaculately groomed receptionist, raised an eyebrow as she buzzed me in.

'Cliff Hardy, I heard you'd retired.' Marcia had the voice all brothel receptionists have—smooth, reassuring, comforting, designed to put the punters at their ease.

'I'm making a comeback. Is Ruby available?'

'Upstairs, just follow your nose if that's the only thing sticking out.'

The décor at Ruby's is muted plush. The stairs are carpeted, the handrail is polished and the mirror at the first landing is set at a flattering angle. I went down a corridor to Ruby's office. Music was playing inside—classical, which is as far as I could get to identifying it. I knocked and went in.

Ruby retired from active service years ago, but she has maintained her face and figure with a certain amount of surgical help. She was working at a computer and swung around on her chair.

'Cliff, darling. It's been a long time.'

She got up and came towards me, moving well, and elegant in a loose satin shirt and tight pants. In her heels she was almost as tall as me. She hugged me and stepped back.

'Older,' she said. 'And wiser?'

'Don't know about that.'

She groped me gently. 'Hornier? I live in hope.'

'Couldn't spoil a beautiful friendship.'

She sighed theatrically. 'Business, as always. Have a seat.' She turned a knob on the portable CD player beside the computer and the music subsided to a whisper. 'Haydn,' she said. 'You look a bit grim, Cliff. At a guess you've just come away from something unpleasant. Drink?'

I nodded. She opened a bar fridge and made two stiff gins and tonic.

'Lime or lemon?'

'You choose.'

She chose lime. We clinked glasses. I handed her the photograph. 'D'you know the girl in the middle, Ruby?'

'I know one of them. First I have to know what trouble they're in.'

'The girl on the right's not in any trouble as far as I know. The one on the left is dead. The one in the middle is my concern. Mary Oberon. She's done some iffy things but nothing too serious, I don't think. She's involved in something I'm working on and she's been threatened. I want to know who by because that might tell me who put her up to the things she's done that have brought her to my attention. I don't mean her any harm.'

'You never do, but it goes along with the work you do, right?'

I didn't respond. She had it exactly.

Ruby worked on her drink, still studying the photograph. 'I've got it now. She's involved in that Bobby Forrest thing that's been all over the tabloids. So are you. You don't think she killed him?'

'She didn't.'

'But she knows who did?'

'I think so. The African-looking girl said she knew. She implied Mary Oberon had told her. I went to see her and found her dead.'

Ruby raised her glass in a sort of salute. 'I didn't know her. The other one goes by the name of Isabella. She's from the islands somewhere.'

'Mary Oberon is a Fijian-Indian, I think.'

'Yeah, partly anyway. You can't find her?'

I took a good pull on the drink and shook my head. 'I traced her to where some guy threatened her and that was it. Any idea where she might have gone?'

'No. Back home?'

'The African girl said she was illegally here. If Mary Oberon's the same it'd be tricky to leave. The cops are looking for her, too. What about Isabella? She might be in danger as well if she knows what the African girl knew. Any ideas about her?'

Ruby finished her drink. She used a long fingernail to spike the slice of lime and ate it. 'You wouldn't dob them in to Immigration would you, Cliff?'

'I might threaten to, but I wouldn't do it.'

She laughed. 'You're an honest man, Cliff Hardy. Don't meet many, especially in this game. All I can tell you is where Isabella works and probably these other girls as well. Place called Black Girls. It's in Double Bay.'

'Nice place?'

'Not very, from what I hear.'

'What else d'you hear?'

'That it's got high-level protection.'

'Who from?'

She shrugged. 'Hard to say, but you'd better be careful.'

I thanked her for the information and the drink and left. I heard the music surge up as I walked towards the stairs.

Black Girls had a website. It emphasised the exotic nature of its 'ladies' and promised luxurious and unusual settings as well as an outcall service. I waited until 9 pm before I called.

'Black Girls, good evening.'

'Is Miranda available tonight?'

'I'm afraid Miranda is no longer with us, sir.'

'How about Isabella?'

'I'm afraid Isabella has commitments tonight, but I'm sure we . . .'

I hung up. I drove to Double Bay and located the place a block from New South Head Road. I circled the block. Black Girls occupied a freestanding terrace that had undergone a lot of renovation—high cement wall with a security gate, new-looking tiled roof, side and back balconies with views of the water. Whatever had stood next to it as a pair had gone and the space had become a private parking area with a boom gate. Space for several cars, two in position.

I parked on the opposite side of the street three houses away under a spreading plane tree. There was a street light and I had a good view of the establishment. Over the next few hours the operational pattern became clear. Cars pulled out of the parking area with a woman sitting in the back seat. I followed one trip. The driver deposited a tall, slender black woman at an address in Point Piper. He waited for a little over an hour and drove her drove back to Double Bay. Back at the brothel, I followed the next car to leave. It took its passenger, a woman with a more than passing resemblance to Naomi Campbell, to a house in Randwick. The driver settled himself behind the wheel and opened a magazine.

I waited until he seemed immersed. I approached, opened the front passenger door and sat with the .38 held low, pointing up at him. He yelped and dropped the magazine. It fell open in his lap showing a double-page picture of a naked woman with enormous breasts.

'Hands on the wheel,' I said. 'Stay very still and very quiet and you won't get hurt. Do anything else and you get hurt, so does the girl and I take her money and this car. Understand?'

He nodded.

'You take the girls back to their places sometimes, right?'

'S . . . sometimes, yeah.'

'Where do you keep the addresses?'

He gulped. 'Glove box.'

One of his hands moved and I brought the barrel of the pistol down hard on the knuckles. Keeping the gun very steady I opened the glove box with my left hand, felt inside and took out a slim notebook.

'This it?'

'Yeah.'

'What's the name of the woman you just dropped off?'

'Naomi.'

'Figures. Where does Naomi live?'

'I dunno.' He nodded at the book. 'I'd have to look it up in there.'

'Okay. You've been smart so far. Let's see if you can stay smart. I'm going. You sit still and look at the tit pictures. You can wank away if you want to. Don't say anything about this to anyone. You get the addresses from one of the other drivers and no one needs to know what happened here. Right?'

It was taking too long and I was talking too much. He made a sudden grab at the gun but he wasn't quick enough. I bent my arm to take the gun out of his reach, then whipped it back and hit his windpipe hard with my elbow. He let out a high-pitched screech and scrabbled frantically at his neck as he tried to suck in air. I got out, walked back to my car and drove off.

I drove to a wine bar I knew in Double Bay and ordered a glass of red. It came with a glass of water and a bowl of nuts. I couldn't remember when I'd last eaten so I ate all the nuts. I drank the water, sipped the wine and opened the notebook. The handwriting was large and round, easy to read. Miranda was there at Baxter Street, Bondi; Simisola was there at Little Seldon Street, Paddington. Isabella's address was a flat at 29 View Street, Coogee. I drank the wine slowly and drove to Coogee. The block of flats was small and new with sophisticated security. There was no way to tell when Isabella would discharge her commitments. I was tired. I drove home.

I turned on the late news. There was a shot of the Little Seldon Street house and a brief report. A woman had been found dead with evidence of foul play. The police called on the person who'd reported finding the body to come forward and help with their inquiries. No name was given. No details were given of her age or appearance. A Muslim prostitute was super-sensitive territory in the current climate. I wondered whether the police would continue to suppress the information. Probably.

I locked the gun away and put the money in its envelope under my pillow. I was sleeping deeply but dreaming a lot. My dreams were all of women—some white, some black, some beautiful, some not. Some of them made sexual advances to me and I responded but they faded away before anything could happen. Jane Devereaux came to me with a letter she said would tell me who killed Bobby but it was in mirror writing and I couldn't read it.

12

Prostitutes tend not to be drivers. They get driven a lot and many of them have drugs in their possession or in their system, making it not worth the risk of being pulled over. They also tend to get up late after a hard night's work, but I was outside the View Street flats at 8.30 am just in case.

Isabella ran true to form. No car and she didn't show until well after ten o'clock. Visually, she was worth waiting for: her brown skin seemed to glow in the early sunlight and her dark hair had the sort of sheen you see in television commercials. She wore a short, leopard-print jacket and loose black trousers, high heels. She walked with a dancer's grace and the only men who didn't stare at her were those looking the other way. She strode off towards the main drag, smoking, with a bag matching her jacket slung over her shoulder. I followed her.

The morning was mild with a light wind and the tang of the sea in the air. The early rush had subsided and there weren't many people about—a few joggers, a few pram pushers, a few oldsters sitting under cover in the park. Isabella was at an outside café table. She butted the cigarette she was smoking and immediately lit another. She gave her order and sat back looking at the water. She was the only person in the café's outside area. She took a mobile phone from her bag and made a call. She laughed, showing gleaming white teeth. I moved up quietly and sat across the table from her. I put the photograph on the table beside her bag.

'Don't be alarmed. I don't mean you any harm. I have to talk to you. It's about your friend Miranda, and this woman.'

She was older than she'd looked at a distance and from the way she moved. She was handsome rather than beautiful, but striking. She looked at the photo and blew some smoke, unperturbed at being accosted.

'Simisola,' she said in a New Zealand accent. 'I suppose you're a cop.'

'No.' I gave her my card. She glanced at it.

'Even worse. What do you want?'

Her coffee arrived. Black. She tore the top off three packets of Equal and poured them into the cup. Her long nails were painted silver.

'You haven't heard the news this morning, have you? Or seen the paper?'

'Baby, I don't watch the news or read the paper. It's all bad stuff.'

'Simisola's dead.'

She stirred her coffee. 'Silly bitch. I suppose one of her crazy brothers got her.'

'I don't know. She rang me yesterday. She said she had information for sale. But you're right, she mentioned honour killing.'

She drank some coffee and finished her cigarette in two long draws. She snuffed it out and gave me a full candlepower smile. 'I have three to start the day and that's it. What information?'

'Something about Miranda.'

'What were you looking for—a three-way plus one? No, you're on about something serious. Bound to be pain.'

I gave her a severely edited version of my interest in Miranda. She drank her coffee and listened without expression.

'They're both silly bitches, Miranda and Simisola. Miranda's always looking for something extra, like an angle, a big score. Simisola was on a real good thing with that Muslim bit.'

'How do you mean?'

'She used to wear the head rag for the punters.'

'Muslim men?'

'And others. You'd be surprised at what turns blokes on.' She gave me the smile again. 'Or maybe you wouldn't. So she didn't sell you the information?'

'No.'

'What was it?'

'I don't know. I hoped it was how to find Miranda.'

She felt in her bag for her cigarettes.

'I thought you said you only had three,' I said.

'I need to think. Order some more coffee.'

A few other people had taken their places at the tables and the waitress was in and out of the café. I ordered two more long blacks. Isabella lit up and waited for the coffee. It came and she did the thing with the sweetener.

'How much trouble is Miranda in?'

Much the same question Ruby asked. Solidarity. I shrugged. 'Nothing at all from me, a bit from the police, some from people she's got involved with. All I want is answers to a few questions.'

'And you'll pay for the answers?' She glanced at the card. 'Cliff?'

I drank some coffee but I'd let it cool too much. I pushed the cup away. 'Yes.'

'Will you pay me to tell you where Miranda is, or where she might be?'

I nodded.

'How much?'

'Five hundred.'

'A grand.'

'Split the difference—seven fifty.'

'I can get that for one trick.'

I looked closely at her. There was a suggestion of a double

chin and the lines around her eyes were spreading. 'Not anymore,' I said.

She dropped her butt in the dregs of the coffee. 'You're right, but you're a shit to say so. Okay, seven fifty. Let's see it first.'

I took the notes from my wallet. Seven hundreds, one fifty. She hesitated.

'Her name's not really Miranda.'

'I know, it's Mary Oberon.'

'Fuck, I was hoping for the other two fifty. In fact it's Oberoi. She figured Oberon was classier. She's got a brother named Ramesh. He runs a restaurant up on the central coast. She used to talk about working there. How she liked it. I mean working in the restaurant.'

'Indian restaurant?'

'What do you reckon?'

'Where on the central coast?'

'Fucking stupid name for a place—Woy Woy.'

I handed her the money.

'Say hello for me,' she said.

There were several Indian restaurants in Woy Woy and one of them was named Ramesh's. At one time I had a girlfriend who lived near Newcastle and I spent a bit of time up there with her. But I wouldn't have detoured to visit the central coast for many years. I surfed up there when I was younger.

In those days we used to drive up in old cars with our boards on the roof and an esky full of beer. This time I decided to take the train. Get around by taxi. Hope Isabella's tip was right. Stay overnight.

I packed a bag and caught a train to Wyong from Central Station. I settled down with C.J. Sansom's *Heartstone*. I'd been working my way through his Tudor series. Good reads, although this one was a bit slow—padded, as a lot of novels are now. I don't know why. I looked out the window from time to time but basically let the kilometres take care of themselves. No food or drink on City Rail trains. I had a flask of scotch in my bag in case of delays and emergencies.

The train was held up for almost an hour just out of Berowra. Signals malfunction they called it, which is not what you want to hear. It was late afternoon by the time the train got to Woy Woy. A taxi took me to a motel in the centre of town. I'd printed out a town map from the web. Ramesh's North Indian restaurant was only a block away. I consulted the phone directory but there was no Oberoi listed residentially, so it had to be the restaurant. Well, nothing wrong with a good rogan josh after a train trip. I rang the restaurant and booked for one at seven thirty.

I took a walk around the town centre to get the stiffness out of my legs and back. Woy Woy is a sort of generic Australian coastal town; could be Nowra, could be Ulladulla, could be Coffs Harbour. There was the usual run of shops with a Coles and a Woolworths and the inevitable McDonald's and KFC. All I knew about the town was that it had once been a fishing village and Spike Milligan's parents had lived there and Spike spent a bit of time there himself. There were worse places to be and I was willing to bet that anything with a view of the water would be pricey.

I walked past the restaurant, saw it was both licensed and BYO. I bought a bottle of Eaglehawk chardonnay at a bottle shop. Ramesh's was an upmarket place with muted lighting and gleaming white tablecloths. The Indian décor had been kept low-key and tasteful. It was more than half full even at that comparatively early hour.

The customers were being shown to their seats by a plump woman in a sari. When it was my turn she looked around the room and made a gesture of despair.

'I'm terribly sorry, sir. You will have to wait a few minutes for your table. Please sit at the bar and have a drink on the house. My apologies.'

'That's quite all right,' I said. 'Seating one can be awkward.'

'Not usually, but there is a big concert on tonight and people are eating early. I'll put your wine on the ice.'

She escorted me to the bar, spoke briefly to the barman and drifted away. I ordered a gin and tonic and looked around the room. It was the kind of place Lily Truscott and I used to like—medium expensive, good service and, I assumed, no sitar music. Eating alone was one of the things that triggered memories of Lily, who'd been murdered three years before. I sipped the drink and recalled Ray Frost's question, *Did you get even?* I'd got even with Lily's killer but it hadn't helped. I still missed her.

There was a mirror behind the bar and I saw my face set in a kind of angry scowl. I drank some more gin and tried to change the expression.

'Your table is ready, sir.'

The woman smiling at me wore a blue and silver sari. She smelled of something fragrant and her voice was musical. The sari, the jewel in her nose, the filigree headband and the spot of red on her forehead made a difference, but it was still Mary Oberon.

13

She showed me to a table in the corner, one of a set of tables for two slightly screened off from the body of the restaurant to allow intimacy. She smiled and walked away. A waiter arrived with a menu and we went through the ritual. I ordered the meal and he brought the wine in an ice bucket. The room was pleasantly warm and I took off my jacket. The entree samosas with the dips were tasty, the papadums were crisp and the meat dish was hot without being fiery. A couple of different chutneys and jasmine rice. It was served smoothly and efficiently and when I indicated I'd pour my own wine the waiter left me to it.

I watched Mary Oberon as she glided around the room. She took people to their tables and performed small functions to help the waiters and the cashier. She appeared to enjoy the work and to be good at it. But there was something a little off-centre about her behaviour—as if she were acting the part rather than being completely at home in it. The soft light flattered her and she appeared younger than in the posed picture Bobby had shown me. Younger, exotic and something else—wary?

Within an hour people began to drift off, presumably to the concert, so that Mary Oberon and the waiters became less busy. I ate slowly, hoping still more people would leave so that I might be able to attract and hold her attention for a while. I had two glasses of wine and poured a third. A waiter came over and asked me if I wanted dessert.

'No, thanks. Just a long black coffee. And could you ask Mary to come and have a word with me, please.'

He looked surprised but he went to where she was standing and spoke to her. She came over, still smiling but even more wary-looking.

'Is there something wrong, sir?'

I returned the smile, tried to look non-threatening. 'No, I'd like to talk to you. It's about Bobby Forrest.'

The calm poise fell away. She stared at me as if I'd spat in her face. The table had been set for two. She grabbed a knife and stabbed at my throat. I jerked up and sideways and the blade hit me in the right shoulder. It went through my shirt and in beside the collarbone. I sat, more surprised than hurt. She turned and ran, silver shoes slapping the tiled floor. The knife didn't have much of a point and didn't go in far. I pulled it out easily and blood welled and flowed. It soaked my shirt and dripped onto the table. The plump woman and a waiter appeared and blocked the view of the remaining diners.

I grabbed a napkin and pressed it to the wound. It was soggy with blood inside a few seconds.

'Come with me, sir,' the woman said. 'We have a doctor. He will help you.'

They led me through a door a few steps away.

'Fetch Ahmed and some towels quickly,' the woman said to the waiter. She took me down a short passage to an office and sat me in a chair. The blood had stopped flowing but the shoulder was throbbing and the arm felt stiff.

The waiter appeared with a couple of snowy white towels, followed by a man in a chef's uniform.

'This is my brother Ahmed,' the woman said. 'He is a doctor.'

I nodded and let him tear the shirt away.

'My bag,' he said.

He was in his thirties and very composed. He used a towel to wipe away most of the blood and pressed it against the wound which was seeping slightly. He glanced at me as he worked.

'I do not think you are in shock.'

'No,' I said.

'You have been hurt before perhaps?'

'A few times, yes.'

The waiter returned with a medical bag. He opened it, took out alcohol swabs and cleaned the wound.

'No nerve damage, I think, but stitching will be necessary.'

'I'd better get to a hospital then.'

He exchanged alarmed looks with the woman.

'Dr Oberoi could do it,' she said.

She sounded very nervous. Advantage Hardy.

'You seem to have some problems,' I said.

'Yes.'

'This is a serious assault.'

'Yes.'

'A . . . hysterical daughter and a brother practising medicine without a licence.'

'Do you want me to stitch this wound or not?'

'Just a minute, doctor. I'm willing to allow you to stitch and I won't report the assault on one condition.'

The woman clasped her heavily ringed hands together. 'What is that?'

'You have to make Mary talk to me. I just want information from her. It's not information she'll want to give but I have to have it. If you can make that clear to her and she'll tell me what I need to know, none of this has to cause you any trouble. I don't think anyone in the restaurant noticed anything.'

'Very well. I will see to it.'

'Stitch away, doctor,' I said.

Various members of the family lived in three flats above the restaurant. They took me up there and into a small room which Ahmed Oberoi obviously used as a surgery when he wasn't cooking curries. He stitched me up, applied some cream and bandaged my shoulder. As he worked he told me he'd fully qualified as a doctor in India but hadn't been able to satisfy the Australian medical authorities.

'It was when there was all the fuss about Dr Haneef,' he said. 'There was a lot of prejudice.'

I nodded. Kevin Andrews had a lot to answer for.

He seemed perfectly competent to me. He disapproved when I asked for whisky and painkillers but his sister obliged. She apologised profusely for what had happened and expressed her undying gratitude to me for not reporting the incident.

'It would be a disaster for the business,' she said. 'There is a lot of competition and a lot of prejudice as Ahmed says.'

'We have an arrangement,' I said.

'I have sent someone to bring her here. It will not take long. You will be gentle with her.'

'Yes. Has she . . . behaved violently like this before?'

She shook her head. 'Not in such a way, no. But she was very distressed when she came from Sydney. She seems to be under great pressure but she will not say why.'

'You asked her why?'

'Of course, but she will say nothing. We have been very worried. In a way perhaps it is good that you are here. Perhaps we will learn something.'

Mrs Oberoi checked my name. She took me into a sitting

room and offered tea which I refused in favour of more whisky. They brought Mary in about an hour later. The sari, headband, nose jewel and caste mark were gone. She wore boots, jeans and a sweater and her hair was tied up in a knot. No makeup. Her mother spoke to her in what I took to be Hindi. Mary nodded and her mother left.

'I'm sorry,' she said, 'I panicked.'

'I'll mend. Your uncle did a great job. I know you've been scared. I know about the man who tried to run you down in Burwood.'

'Then you know all about . . . what do you know?'

Mrs Oberoi had brought my jacket to the room. I reached into the pocket with my right hand without thinking and grimaced at the pain. I used my left hand and took out the photograph of her that Bobby had given me and the one I'd found in Simisola's house.

'You know a lot,' she said. 'How much have you told my mother?'

'Nothing and I've got no reason to. What I don't know is who put you up to contacting Bobby and harassing him when he didn't respond.'

She shook her head. 'I can't tell you that.'

'You have to. Otherwise I report this,' I touched my shoulder, 'to the police. You're in trouble and your uncle is in trouble.'

'You're a bastard. If you found me, they can find me.'

'Your choice. How did you keep your family from knowing what you did in Sydney?'

'They don't read the papers or watch television. They just work, night and day.'

She reached for the whisky bottle, uncapped it and took a swig. The hard shell she'd needed in Sydney was forming again.

'You know Simisola's dead. Did that have anything to do with you?'

'No. How did you find me?'

'Isabella.'

She laughed. 'How much?'

'Seven fifty.'

'Cheap. How much are you offering me?'

'I'm offering you my silence.'

'They're good people, my family.'

'They seem to be.'

'I'm the black sheep.'

'So was I.'

'There's a difference. I was born in Fiji and brought up more strictly than you can believe. The only thing on the minds of my mother and father was to save money and get to Australia. They moved heaven and earth to do it. And I had to be good at all times. There couldn't be the slightest thing the immigration Nazis could object to. They applied and waited and waited until the day came.'

I let her tell it her way. I had the feeling she'd give me what I wanted but she had to talk herself into it first.

'My uncle had applied from India and he got here, too. Eventually. But he couldn't practise. That was a blow. The strictness towards me continued but, hey, this is Australia. I wouldn't wear it. I went to Sydney, tried to break into acting, but . . . couldn't. Have you got a cigarette?'

'Sorry, no.'

'Bugger.'

Hard to see why she didn't make it as an actress. She was pretty good. The performance as a demure, exotic Asian restaurant host had been convincing and now she was a convincing tough chick.

'One thing led to another,' she said, 'and I ended up at Black Girls. It wasn't so bad—mostly call-outs to nice places. They keep too much of the money and they watch you like hawks but . . . Anyway, there was this guy who was something to do with the management. He came to me with a proposition.'

'To entrap Bobby Forrest.'

'Yeah. It was a good deal. He bought me a computer and showed me the ropes. It wasn't hard to get under Bobby's skin, believe me.'

'At first.'

'Right, at first. He was very cute and I didn't mind that much that he couldn't get it up. A lot of men can't. There's other ways if they've got any imagination.'

'But Bobby didn't have any imagination.'

'No, he agonised and carried on. I only saw him twice.'

Bobby said once, I thought. They never give you the whole story.

Mrs Oberoi opened the door. 'Is everything all right?'

Mary looked ready to shout at her but she fought the impulse down.

'It's all right,' I said. 'Thank you.'

Mary rubbed her forehead where the red spot had been. 'Then Bobby met that woman and didn't want to have anything to do with me. So I had to keep the pressure on. You know about all that?'

'Yes. Who was this man?'

'I'm afraid to tell you.'

'Why did he want you to do all this?'

'It wasn't for him, it was for his boss. The boss owns the brothel.'

'Why did you go to Burwood?'

'After Bobby got killed and that media stuff about Miranda appeared I panicked. I wiped all the emails and the stuff on the site. He wanted them to send to the bitch Bobby took up with but I was scared to have them on my computer so I wiped them. That freaked this guy. He wanted me to get right away, go to Melbourne. To a brothel down there. I didn't want to go. I hate Melbourne. It's cold and wet and flat and bad things happen there.'

'Bad things happen everywhere. Why Burwood?'

'Burwood was as boring a place as I'd ever been to. I thought I could hide there. But he found me.'

'And threatened you?'

'Big time. I think he would've really hurt me but there was someone watching from across the street.'

'What's his name, Mary? You have to tell me.'

'You'll go away if I do? You won't say anything about this,' she pointed to my shoulder, 'or say that I gave you his name?'

'Right. You have my word.'

'Piss on your word. His name is Alex Mountjoy.'

14

'You know him,' she said.

'I know of him. So he's the one who drove the car at you—bearded, drives a white Commodore?'

'Yes.'

'Do you think he killed Bobby?'

Her eyes opened wide. 'No, why would he do that?'

'His boss seems to have had it in for Bobby.'

She shook her head. 'I think he wanted to make Bobby suffer, not to kill him. Is that what you're on about—finding out who killed Bobby?'

I nodded.

'But you're not a cop.'

Using my left hand again I fished in my jacket for my wallet. Gave her a card.

'Are you working for that woman—the one with the

brains? It really pissed me off, that newspaper stuff. I've got brains, too.'

'It annoyed her as well. It doesn't matter who I'm working for. Do you know where Mountjoy lives?'

'Of course I do. I fucked him there enough times, didn't I?'

'Where?'

She smiled. 'This is extra.'

'It's in your interest for me to deal with him.'

'How do I know you can? All I've seen you do is threaten people.'

'I'll pay you what I paid Isabella, not a cent more.'

'Okay, let's see it.'

I'd anticipated something like this and brought a chunk of Ray Frost's money with me. I selected the right notes and held them just out of her reach.

'He lives directly across the street from Black Girls, so he can keep an eye on things and doesn't have to go far for a fuck.'

I handed the money to her. She tucked it into the pocket of her jeans.

'He's a kick-boxer,' she said. 'I hope he kicks your fucking head in.'

Mrs Oberoi provided me with a T-shirt and offered to call me a cab. I thanked her and told her I could walk and the incident was closed.

'Can you tell me anything about what happened to her in Sydney?' she asked.

How to answer that? How to tell a mother that her daughter was a prostitute and an associate of low-lifes who'd lead her deeper and deeper into trouble unless she was lucky? I realised that people like the Oberois were cut off from many of the realities of Australian life. They worked hard and prospered, they adapted as best they could and sometimes cut corners—as the qualified but unregistered doctor was doing—but they remained innocents in some ways, and vulnerable.

Mary had made a break from 'the life' and had been scared. It was possible that the fear would put her on another path. She knew she faced danger from several quarters. I knew only too well how being linked to a violent death could affect your judgement, your decisions, your future. She'd made the right move in getting clear, and she had a veil of sorts to hide behind. The odds might just be with her. But only just. I couldn't offer the woman much.

'No,' I said, 'but I think she'll get over it.'

Back at the motel I took stock. Now I had a clear suspect for Bobby's murderer and, with Jane Devereaux's information, a background to how and why it might have happened. It had cost me a sore, stiff shoulder but I'd recover. The problem was, it had run me up against a formidable antagonist in Michael Tennyson. There was also no answer to Mary Oberon's question: *Why would he do that?* If it was Mountjoy who caught up with Bobby in Strathfield, perhaps he only meant to scare him. Maybe the death was an accident.

Another couple of painkillers and another whisky saw me off to sleep. I rolled onto the shoulder a few times in the night and woke up swearing. It was one of those nights when dawn couldn't come quickly enough. Washing and dressing were difficult. I envied my grandson Ben, who appeared to be completely ambidextrous, the way my mother had been. I drank instant coffee and waited until it was time to get a taxi to the station.

I bought the papers and settled down with them and C.J. Sansom. Mary Oberon was right—the news was mostly bad unless you owned a lot of mining shares and didn't care about pedophile priests, abusive parents and lying politicians. I read a hundred pages about the machinations in the court of Henry VIII and reflected that things were pretty much the same back then, but with a lot of religious camouflages and stiffer penalties when the truth was revealed. I tried to keep the arm and shoulder moving and it responded pretty well. Not that I was too worried about going up against a kick-boxer even if I wasn't fully fit—a kick-boxer stands no chance against a street fighter. It's the same with karatists.

Train travel aids reflection and recollection. I remember a drinking session I once had with the actor Bill Hunter. I was working as a bodyguard for one of the actors on a film he had a major role in. He was sober for his scenes, but liked to drink afterwards. He'd boxed a bit, sparred with professionals. We had things in common. I drank a fair amount in those days.

'It's a matter of being willing, Cliff,' he said. 'You have to be willing.'

'Willing to do what, Bill?'

'You don't even ask what. Willing to do anything.'

He'd named a couple of actors he knew with the quality, and some London and Sydney crims, most of them dead by that time, and I knew what he meant. It's something that comes over you—a capacity for violence without limit but still with some control. I'd felt it a few times.

I turned my mind to more cerebral matters. I had no evidence and no prospect of getting any that would stand up in a court of law. But if I could prove to my own satisfaction and that of Ray Frost that Mountjoy and Michael Tennyson were involved in Bobby's death, steps could be taken. Frost had offered help and, judging by his background and things he'd said, strict legality wasn't his main priority. Reprisal would appeal to him more.

The key was Jane Devereaux. I'd asked her to contact me if Tennyson had been in touch directly and she hadn't. I got a taxi from Central to Pyrmont and called her business number from the office.

'I'm glad you called,' she said. 'I've been wondering what to do.'

'What's happened?'

'Nothing really. Nothing direct, but the gifts have kept coming. Not as extravagant, but disturbing.'

'In what way?'

'I'll have to call you back. I can't talk freely in the office. I'll call in ten minutes.'

I dealt with some emails and bills of no importance while I waited. It was closer to twenty minutes before she rang.

'Sorry,' she said. 'I was held up, we're very busy just now.'

I was encouraged by how calm she sounded because she'd need to be to agree to the suggestion I was planning to make.

'The gifts,' she said. 'Lingerie, magazines and DVDs. All very suggestive—pornographic, really, and I'm not easily shocked. In fact I'm not shocked, just . . . disturbed.'

'I understand. How were these things delivered?'

'Not posted, by hand into my box at the flat.'

'Did you do anything about the security?'

'I did and my neighbour told me she thought someone tried to get in one day. And I have a feeling I'm being followed. I'm worried, Mr Hardy, and I don't have anyone else . . .'

'It's all right, I'll help you. We'd better meet and talk things over.'

'Have you made any progress?'

'I think so. Your office is in Surry Hills, isn't it? Can we meet around there after you finish work?'

She named a wine bar in Crown Street within walking distance of her office and we arranged to meet at 6 pm. I planned to be in Riley Street across from her office a good bit earlier. If she was being followed things could take an interesting turn.

I parked behind the library in Crown Street, took up a position and watched. She wasn't followed. She walked briskly in her high heels, wearing a dark suit and carrying the usual briefcase. I caught up with her at the door to the wine bar.

'Hello,' I said. 'You'll be glad to hear you weren't followed. What can I get you?'

'A glass of red, please.'

Good choice after a hard day's work. I got two glasses of the house red and we sat where I could keep an eye on whoever came in. She looked tired, as though she was lacking sleep, but perhaps it was just long hours at the desk late in the week. The wine was smooth and she drank half the glass in a couple of quick pulls.

I told her what Bobby had said about her making him feel better than he was, and how Ray Frost had echoed the words in his eulogy. She smiled and had some more wine. 'I'm drinking more than I did,' she said.

'Understandable.'

She didn't turn heads, but there was something about her manner, the way she sat, her composure, that drew attention. I told her about my meeting with Mary Oberon without mentioning the knife.

'How did you get her to tell you that?'

'I applied moral pressure.'

She smiled and some of the tired look fell away. 'I've no idea what you mean, but do you think now that Alexander Mountjoy killed Bobby?'

'I'm not sure, but he's the prime candidate.'

'Can you go to the police?'

'No, there's no proof. I want to ask you to do something, if you're willing.'

'That sounds ominous.' She emptied her glass and got up. 'I'm going to need another drink. How about you?'

I nodded.

'Watch my briefcase, please.'

The place had filled up and she had to wait to be served. She spoke to a couple of people. It was obviously the watering hole for publishers. One of the men tried to engage her but she smiled and shook her head. He looked disappointed. She returned with two glasses and a small carafe. She poured.

'What do you want me to do?'

'Contact Michael Tennyson.'

'Jesus. You don't mean meet him?'

'No, I want you to say you're returning his gifts and that he has no chance with you because you have someone else in your life now.'

'I don't follow.'

'If you agree, I want us to go around together. Like now, and go to other places. If Tennyson has someone following you he'll see us together. Even if he doesn't he'll find out in some way. He has the contacts.'

'Yes, I'm sure he has. But why?'

'If he sent Mountjoy after Bobby he'll very likely send him after me.'

We both drank some wine. She dipped a finger in the wine and drew circles on the table. Her nails were short, unpainted but well cared for. She looked up and examined me as if she was seeing me for the first time. She saw greying but thick hair, weather-beaten skin and a nose shaped by other men's fists. No oil painting but not a gargoyle either.

'You mean we'd have to appear to be lovers?'

'Something like that.'

She nodded. 'You're a bit old for me, but I think I could make it look convincing.'

15

We kept it up for ten days. We went to dinner three or four times, met for lunch a couple of times and I stayed over at her flat, sleeping on the couch, two nights, and she spent one night in my spare room. I drove her to work on two mornings. She took my arm in the street sometimes. After a week she phoned Tennyson and told him there was a new man in her life.

'He was furious,' she said. 'He called me foul names and said he'd make you sorry you were ever born.'

'Good.'

'Aren't you afraid?'

'No. I've had a lot of experience at dealing with threats and threateners.'

'I believe you. What happened to your shoulder?'

I'd tried not to show any sign of the injury but she'd picked it up. I told her and she made a face.

'We caused a lot of trouble, Robert and I, didn't we?'

'None of it your fault, Jane.'

It was all very strange. I'd never had a platonic relationship with a woman before. I enjoyed her company. She was very intelligent and had a sense of humour. Her flat was crammed with books—mostly history and biography, a few of which I'd read. Her taste in fiction was more highbrow than mine, but she had a scattering of good lighter stuff. We talked books a bit and politics. She was editing a biography of William John MacKay, the policeman who pulled Francis de Groot from his horse after he'd slashed the ribbon to mark the opening of the Sydney Harbour Bridge. MacKay went on to become Commissioner of Police. It sounded like the sort of book I'd read and she was interesting about it.

We played it straight, no flirtation. She was still grieving for Bobby and she was right—she was much too young for me and, anyway, something serious was at stake. I enjoyed it, but it did leave me acutely aware of my singleness.

Megan spotted us at dinner in Newtown and rang me the next day.

'Who is she, Cliff?'

'A client.'

'Nothing more? You seemed very friendly.'

'Nothing more.'

'Are you sure? She was giving you the look.'

'What look?'

'The look a woman gives a bloke when she's getting interested in him.'

'No chance of that.'

'I worry about you. You should be looking for someone.'

'I'm always looking for someone, it's my job.'

'That's right, joke—but too long on your own and you'll dry up, get set in bachelor ways. Before long you'll be washing your underwear in the bathroom basin and wearing your socks for a week.'

'Is that what bachelors do?'

'Yes.'

'How would you know?'

'I've read about it.'

'I'll try to remember it, love, but if it'll set your mind at rest there is someone I'm hoping to catch up with when I've finished this job.'

'Sounds as if you're making it up.'

'No. She's a singer. I've got her CD somewhere. I'll lend it to you.'

'Wow!'

A couple of times as we went about our phony courtship I had the feeling that we were under surveillance. But it was a fleeting feeling, hard to be certain and not something I could act on. I was sure we were followed on the roads twice, but as soon as I took action designed to draw the driver closer or trap him, he peeled off. A white Commodore. The second time Jane noticed.

'We were being followed, weren't we?'

'Yes.'

'You didn't try to get away.'

'No, I tried to let the car get closer to have a better look at the driver.'

'But?'

'He twigged to what I was doing.'

'This isn't working, is it?'

'Not as well as I hoped. Wait on, he's back. Jane, I want to try something drastic. Just do exactly as I say, okay?'

She nodded.

We'd had dinner in Randwick. I drove back to her place, parked outside and escorted her up the path. The car that had followed us cruised slowly into view. Halfway to the entrance doors I grabbed her and kissed her.

'Shove me away hard and hit me,' I said.

She did it. I slapped her quite solidly, held her and slapped again, trying to make the second slap look harder but pulling it. I swung her around and pushed her down without letting her fall. I kept a firm grip and dragged her to the entrance, pretending to shout at her.

'Struggle,' I said.

She struggled.

We got to the entrance, where we couldn't be seen from the street and I put my arms around her.

'I'm sorry,' I said. 'I'm trying to provoke something. It was the only way. Are you all right?'

She was breathless and hung on to me for a minute before breaking away.

'I'm all right. It hurts a bit. I'd hate to be hit by you if you meant it.'

'You're terrific, Jane, just terrific. Go in now. I'll ring you tomorrow. I'm hoping this'll bring things to a head.'

She put her hand to the side of her face. 'Be careful,' she said.

I waited until she had gone inside and then I came out and walked back to my car. There was no movement in the street. I drove back to Glebe as slowly as I could. I wasn't followed. I gave myself a physical check as I drove. I was still stiff and sore in various spots and there was no point in pretending I was the fighter I'd once been. But I was still strong and quick and could put up a good show at least for a short spell. And most street fights are over within seconds. I'd been in quite a few and seen others and never one that lasted as long as they do in the movies.

He was waiting for me as I suspected he would be. It was late and the street was quiet. The white Commodore was parked four or five car spaces from my house. I stripped off the light jacket I was wearing as I got out of the car. I approached my gate and he stepped out from behind my neighbour's giant

4WD. The spot isn't well lit, but it was light enough for me to see that he was big and bulky with a prominent jaw and a beard.

'You're going to be sorry you were ever born, arsehole,' he said.

'You're repeating what your boss said. Don't you have any ideas of your own?'

That annoyed him, which was his first mistake. He rushed at me. I stepped aside and almost tripped him but he was nimble and got his balance back before I could hit him. He got in one straight punch to my still tender shoulder and I gasped and had to step back. That encouraged him and he made his second mistake. Kick-boxers think they have an extra weapon but they don't really. As soon as they swing that foot their balance is a factor and in the ring their opponents aren't permitted to grab hold. I was waiting for the kick. It came and if it had landed it would have done serious damage. He wore a pair of heavy boots, but that was another mistake. He'd have trained and competed in light shoes and the boots slowed him and affected his timing just a little. Just enough. I caught the foot in both hands and twisted hard as his weight came forward. He screamed as his knee ligaments and tendons stretched and tore and he went down. His head hit a brick pillar and he flopped onto his back. His eyes rolled up and closed.

It had only taken a few seconds and was quiet apart from his yell. I grabbed a handful of his shirt and coat collar and pulled him through my gate and up onto the porch. He was stirring but he wasn't going anywhere with that knee and a probable concussion. I hauled him through the door, dragged him inside and shut the door. He tried to stand and gasped as his weight went onto the knee. He didn't seem to know quite what had happened and he let me half carry him down the passage and drop him into an armchair.

His thick hair had protected his head, but blood was oozing out and trickling across his forehead. I wet a washcloth in the bathroom, filled a glass with water and brought them to him. I put the cloth up to his head and lifted his hand to hold it there. I put the glass in his other hand and lifted it to his mouth.

'Drink it,' I said.

He was dazed and uncoordinated but he gulped down some of the water and kept the cloth in place. My shoulder hurt where he'd hit me but compared to him I was in very good shape. His leg twitched and he yelped as the knee hurt him. The pain seemed to clear his brain and he stared at me as if he couldn't believe someone so much older had taken him so easily.

'You'd be Alexander Mountjoy,' I said. 'Michael Tennyson's pimp and gofer.'

'Fuck you,' he said.

'We're going to have a talk, Alex, but first I need a drink.'

'My leg's . . .'

'Badly damaged and the longer it stays without treatment the worse it'll be. You might try this new synthetic stuff the footballers go in for. Not sure if it'll work for the medial and the cruciate, but . . .'

'Talk about what?'

'Hang on.'

I went upstairs and got the miniature tape recorder Hank had given me as a birthday present and put it in my pocket. Then I got a bottle of scotch and a couple of glasses from the kitchen. I poured two hefty drinks, gave him one and put my hand in my pants pocket to turn on the recorder.

'Let me get a few things straight. You've been helping Tennyson harass Jane Devereaux—delivering obscene material, following her, and you broke into her flat and stole some letters, right?'

'Fuck you again.'

'The longer it takes, the worse for the leg.'

'Okay, okay, yes. I did what I was told to do. No one got hurt.'

'Why is Tennyson doing this?'

'He's crazy, he's obsessed with the ugly cunt.'

'And you drove your car at Mary Oberon. Was that on Tennyson's instruction, too?'

'Yeah, that bloody whore fucked up. She was supposed to screw Forrest up good and proper, but she wasn't up to it. She was supposed to get photos and she fucked that up.'

'And she wiped the emails.'

'Right, the dumb cunt.'

'Tennyson's an unforgiving employer, eh?'

He didn't respond.

'All right, here's the big one. Why did you shoot Bobby Forrest?'

He'd drunk most of the scotch and was wincing with pain but suddenly his manner changed. He gaped at me.

'What?'

'You heard me.'

'I didn't shoot him.'

'Tennyson said he'd have him killed.'

He shook his head and the movement hurt his leg. 'Look, Tennyson's crazy but he's not that crazy. He'd have got me to beat him up, sure, and I'd have been glad to do it—cocky ponce. But that's all.'

It wasn't what I expected to hear and I had to struggle to control my reaction. The trouble was, I believed him. His surprise and alarm were genuine, no doubt about it.

'You followed him and Jane Devereaux in a white Commodore. Forrest spoke to me just before he was killed and he was being followed by a white Commodore.'

'There's a million fucking white Commodores.'

That was true.

'Tell me what happened tonight.'

He told me that he'd phoned Tennyson and reported that I'd hit Jane Devereaux. Tennyson told him to wait for me and hurt me.

'Kill me?' I said.

'No! Just put you in hospital for a long time.'

'Weren't up to the job, were you?'

'Call an ambulance.'

'I've got a better idea.' I took the tape recorder from my pocket, turned it off, rewound it a bit and hit play.

'. . . *crazy, he's obsessed with the ugly cunt.*'

'Oh, Jesus,' Mountjoy said.

I poured him another drink. 'Got your mobile on you, Alex? You're going to give Tennyson a call.'

'No.'

I pointed to his knee. 'I wouldn't be surprised if there were some bone splinters drifting around in there. Every minute counts.'

16

He made the call and I took the phone.

'This is Cliff Hardy. I think you know who I am.'

'Yes.'

A nicely modulated private school voice.

'I've got Alex Mountjoy here and he's not feeling very well.'

'Oh.'

'Yes. I'm going to play a tape of our conversation. I suggest you listen carefully.'

I played the tape. Mountjoy sweated. He used the wet cloth to wipe his face.

'What do you want?' Tennyson said.

'It's not a question of what I *want*. It's what I demand, what I insist upon. I can make as many copies of this tape as I like and send them where I choose, starting right now. Imagine the TV news, imagine the blogs, imagine the share prices of your companies.'

'Go on.'

'You are not to make any kind of contact with Jane Devereaux. You are not to phone, email or write to her, nor to approach her.'

'You hit her.'

'That was a charade. Mountjoy fell for it and so did you. Have you understood so far?'

'Yes.'

'Think about the restraining order she could get if she used that tape.'

'You've made your point.'

'I'm not finished. You are not to cause her any professional difficulties. I know you have influence in the publishing world. If she runs into any trouble that threatens her position the tape gets distributed. Do you understand?'

'Yes.'

'Same goes for me. Any smell I get of your interference in my affairs and the world learns what a pathetic, bullying prick you are.'

That got to him. His voice took on an edge: 'Is that all?'

'No, you'd better send some people for Alex. We're at my place in Glebe. A couple of paramedics and a tame doctor if you have one. Better bring a gurney and some way he can travel comfortably.'

'I gather you thought I was responsible for Forrest's death.'

'I was wrong there. Do you know who was responsible?'

'No, but whoever it was has my congratulations.'
He hung up. I handed the phone back to Mountjoy.
'He's not happy, Alex.'

They arrived forty-five minutes later—two men in tracksuits with a trolley and another in a business suit with a doctor's bag. I met them at the door and waved them in with my .38 in my hand. The doctor looked startled when he saw the gun; the other two didn't.

'Has he had any medication?' the doctor asked.

'Scotch,' I said.

One of the tracksuited guys sniggered.

I stayed by the door while they made their arrangements. The man who'd sniggered approached me, showing that his hands were empty.

'What did you do to him?'

'Not much. He mostly did it to himself.'

'Good on you, he's a ripe shit.'

Mountjoy yelped and swore a couple of times and gave me a filthy look as he was wheeled past. I watched as they loaded him into the back of a station wagon. Then one of the helpers walked back to Mountjoy's Commodore. I waited by the open door with the pistol behind my back until both cars had gone.

I put the gun away, finished my drink and poured another. I got rid of the bloodstained cloth and sat with the tape recorder in my hand. I ejected the cassette—a tiny object to have such a decisive impact. Sort of decisive. I called Jane.

'It's over,' I said.

'What do you mean, Cliff?'

'Tennyson and Mountjoy weren't behind Bobby's death but I've fixed it so that Tennyson won't bother you again. He won't ever contact you or cause you any professional trouble.'

There was a pause. 'How did you manage that?'

'I applied the right kind of pressure to the right person.'

'That's the answer you gave me once before. It means you won't say.'

'It doesn't matter, Jane. It just means that you can get on with your life without worrying about Tennyson.'

'And without Robert. So you still don't know who killed him?'

'No, but I'll keep looking.'

'However can I thank you, Cliff?'

'Just send me a copy of the book about the top copper.'

part three

17

I had a bad time at the inquest. The coroner made derogatory remarks about my profession and, by implication, about me. He came close to suggesting I'd failed in my duty of care.

Rockwell gave a detailed account of his investigation at that point but ended by admitting that he had no promising leads to follow. The finding was inevitable: Robert Raymond Forrest was killed by a person or persons unknown.

Rockwell approached me after the hearing.

'Still sniffing around, Hardy?'

'Sort of.'

'Still bankrolled by Ray Frost?'

'I wouldn't call it bankrolled, but he's still keen to find out what happened and you blokes obviously haven't got very far.'

'Have you heard the latest theory?'

'What d'you mean?'

'Don't you read the tweets and blogs, keep up with Facebook?'

'No.'

'Better catch up if you want to stay in your game.'

We were walking down Parramatta Road away from the Glebe coronial court. The morgue was in the same building and it was a precinct I'd spent a bit of time in over the years.

'What's the theory?'

Rockwell laughed. 'Publicity stunt gone wrong.'

'Come on.'

'It's the latest thing. You claim you were shot at. Generates publicity, wins sympathy.'

We stopped at the lights. Rockwell pressed the button to allow him to cross.

'That's bullshit,' I said.

The light changed. 'It's as good as anything you're likely to come up with.'

It was an empty feeling. The inquiries I'd made, which had looked promising for a while, had come to nothing. I was still holding a fair bit of Ray Frost's money but without any idea of how to use it. A couple of minor jobs came my way—bodyguarding, money minding, process serving. I went about them efficiently enough but my mind was still on Bobby Forrest. I hadn't asked Mountjoy about it because there didn't seem to be any point, but someone had sent that warning text message. I had no idea who.

I concentrated on getting myself fully fit. People who hire someone like me prefer to see a physical specimen better than themselves. I went to the gym four or five times a week and worked harder. The shoulder healed completely and the small scar was nothing compared to some of the others I had.

'Looking good, Cliff,' Wesley Scott said. 'Who is she?'

'Sorry?' I said.

He chuckled. 'Most guys your age getting themselves in shape are doing it to attract or hold a woman. I'm all for it.'

'No woman, Wes. Just trying to look the part of the capable ready-for-everything private detective.'

'Which you are, my man. Just don't overdo it.'

Work harder, they tell you when you're young and *don't overdo it* when you're older. There's no in between. I tapered off a bit. I was spending too much time on my own—working at trivial jobs, exercising, taking my multifarious medications, living in my head. I could feel it getting me down. And in the background, nagging away, was the knowledge that I'd had a client murdered and didn't seem to be able to do anything about it.

That's how things stood when I got a call from Sophie Marjoram. She told me she was co-producing a film starring one of her clients and that the production was held up because the armourer had got sick.

'You've done it before, I know,' she said. 'Can you help us out, Cliff? It's only for a couple of scenes over a day or two. Good rates. I can arrange the union side of it and the insurance.'

I had done it a couple of times. It's time consuming and ticklish. You have to get permits to use the weapons, arrange the hiring and inspect them very closely to make sure they'll operate the way you want. Sometimes you have to supervise the installation of sugar glass windows or windscreens that'll shatter in the right way. You have to liaise with the special effects and stunt people. And you have to teach the actors to keep their hands away from the parts of the weapons that get hot, even when firing blank ammunition. A bad burn and the production company is up for medical costs and can cause the director's worst headaches—injuries and delay.

The film was a police drama set around Sydney and the scenes I was involved in concerned a shoot-out after a robbery and a shotgun suicide. The shoot-out was pretty straightforward but close work with a shotgun is dangerous and needs care. It was a change from my usual line of work and a chance to relate closely with other people. I threw myself into it and enjoyed the whole thing. The waiting around is boring. 'I spent twenty years as an actor,' Gary Cooper once said. 'That's one year acting and nineteen years waiting to act.' But the money's good. Coop should have added that.

My scenes were near the end of the film and, unusually, they were shooting in sequence, so I was around when the director called it a wrap and I was invited to the wrap party.

The party was held in a house in Wharf Road, Balmain. The house was owned by Sophie's co-producer, not by any of the actors, still less by the writer. It was a big sprawling place that ran down to the water where there was a small jetty. I was told that the producer speed-boated himself to his office in Rose Bay and to as many of his meetings as he could get to by water.

The credits at the end of a film seem to roll forever and the names run into the scores if not over a hundred. Not all of them are invited to the party but a lot are and the house was pretty full by the time I arrived. Going to parties solo isn't much fun and I wasn't planning to be there very long. Have a couple of drinks and something from the catered buffet, chat to the chief stunt man, say hello to the special effects girl who'd helped with the shotgun scene.

They were talking on the ground floor, dancing on the first floor to music I'd never heard and doing other things on the top level. I got a scotch, ate some canapés and wandered about nodding and smiling. I was relieved to find Sophie Marjoram on her own in a corner but not so relieved when I saw how drunk she was. She grabbed my arm and pulled me down into a chair beside her.

'Cliff, darling,' she said. 'Isn't this great? Nicky's so happy.'

'Nicky?'

'The star, the bloody star. My boy. He's over there. Look at him. Is he cool or what?'

I looked where she pointed. A tall, slim young man was leaning against the wall talking earnestly to an older man. He wore a dark suit with a white shirt—no tie and the shirt hung outside his trousers. Cool.

'He looks a lot like Bobby Forrest,' I said.

Her face was flushed and her eyes were sparkling until I said that. Her expression changed as she grabbed a glass from a circulating tray. 'Why'd you have to say that? Why'd you have to bring me down? Poor Bobby, he could've had all this. He was better than that . . .'

She was speaking too loudly, possibly loudly enough for the young actor to hear, so I put my hand on her mouth.

'Shush, Soph, too loud. You'll do yourself out of your commission.'

She grabbed my hand and held it in a sweaty grip. 'You think I only care about money. I don't. I love them. I love 'em all, 'specially poor Bobby.'

A young woman in jeans and a silk shirt stained by red wine and with the sleeves rolled up to reveal some interesting tattoos on her left wrist, came across and almost jostled Sophie aside. She was drunk.

'Heard you talking about Bobby Forrest,' she said.

'Yes.'

'What was he to you?'

'Sorry, that's my business. Who are you?'

'I'm Chloe.'

'Chloe what?'

'Just Chloe, just poor Chloe. You shouldn't talk about him, not worth talking about.'

Sophie bristled and Chloe looked ready to get physical when we were interrupted.

I'd been introduced to Earl Carlswell, the director, when I arrived. He came across now and spoke quietly.

'Sophie's not herself,' he said. 'She's had some bad news. I wonder if you'd be kind enough to take her home?'

Sophie was still gripping my hand and trying to get her head onto my shoulder. Her makeup was smeared and her loose top threatened to slide down and reveal more of her than she'd have wanted. I helped her to her feet and she draped herself around me.

'You're nice,' she said. 'Let's have a drink together.'

'Let's not,' I said.

I scooped up her bag, slung it over her shoulder and guided her towards the nearest door. The cool night air and the breeze sobered her up enough to at least walk. The street was full of cars generated by the party and I'd had to park a couple of streets away. She was staggering by the time we reached the car and had to steady herself against it. She took a flask from her bag and had a swig.

'You've had enough, Soph,' I said.

'Fuck you, or is that what you've got in mind?'

I opened the door and helped her in. She took another swig and slumped down in the seat. I got the car moving and realised I didn't know her address.

'I'll take you home, Soph. What's the address?'

She told me. It was Paddington, not far from her office. The traffic was heavy in Darling Street and the going was slow.

'What's the bad news?' I said.

'What?'

'Earl what's-his-name said you'd had some bad news.'

'That prick.' She slurred the words. 'Told me he was cutting Nicky's scenes to the bone. Prick. Nicky'll be devastated, prob'ly blame me. Prick. They never forgive you, actors. Bastards.'

'Who was the drunk girl? I thought I recognised her from somewhere.'

'Chloe? Nobody. Actor groupie. Bit of a nutter.'

She used the flask again and sat silently for the rest of the drive. Something was nagging at me as I navigated Paddington's narrow streets and I nailed it down just as I drew up outside Sophie's house. It was something she'd said in our interview before Bobby was killed. *No, something she hadn't said about his past.* Breaking my old habit, I hadn't made notes on the conversation and, in the drama of the events that followed, it had slipped my mind. I was sure I'd missed something then.

I helped her from the car to her door but she was too drunk to open it. I fished in her bag for the keys and unlocked the door. The house was single-storeyed which was a relief—I didn't fancy carrying her upstairs. I considered trying to get some coffee into her and asking her again about the violent incident but I remembered that she'd been adamant about there being no dirty linen. She was too drunk anyway.

I helped her down the passage to her bedroom. Like her office, it was a mess, clothes lying around on the bed and on other surfaces. I stumbled over shoes as I eased her towards the bed and lowered her down. She was barely conscious. I took off her shoes, lifted her legs onto the bed and made her comfortable. Her eyes opened and she looked at me as if she'd never seen me before. Then her eyes closed and she snored.

I went through to the kitchen and filled a glass with water. I put it on the bedside table. I walked back towards the door and noticed the set of framed photographs along the wall. Men and women, actors; I recognised two—Bobby Forrest and Nicky. I looked at Bobby's picture. It was a studio portrait presenting him in the best possible way. He looked handsome and wholesome, but was he? I thought about Jane Devereaux and Ray Frost and the feeling of failure that had been with me for weeks.

I went back to the bedroom. Sophie had rolled slightly so that she was on her side with one hand up close to her face, probably her natural sleeping position. At a guess she'd be asleep for at least a couple of hours before her bladder or her dry mouth woke her. I juggled her keys in my hand and knew what I had to do.

18

It was quicker to walk the couple of blocks to Sophie's office than to drive there and waste time looking for a park. I tried a few of the keys on the ring until I found the right one. I unlocked the door. There'd been no alarm when Sophie had unlocked it before so it didn't seem likely she'd have had one installed in the interim.

Her office was in the usual mess with scripts and magazines and books piled up everywhere. Sophie had been in the business a long time and, like me, would have kept hard-copy files on her clients. It was a difficult habit to break. There were three filing cabinets. I found the drawers containing the client files in the second cabinet. Chaotic though the office itself was, the files were in strict alphabetical order. It's the only way.

Robert 'Bobby' Forrest's file was thick, running to several bulging folders. He'd only been on Sophie's books for a few years but work in the film business evidently generates a lot of paper—contracts, correspondence, financial statements, magazine and newspaper cuttings. I took the folders to the desk, cleared away the detritus, and began to work systematically through the material.

Most of it was easily set aside. It looked as though his career had started slowly, survived a few glitches and then settled into a pattern of steady improvement. Good stuff for his biographer if there was to be one for such a short life. There probably would be one if the lives of James Dean and Heath Ledger were any guide. I found what I was wondering about in a batch of correspondence and accompanying documents beginning almost four years ago and running for several months.

Bobby Forrest had got into a fight with Jason Clement, another actor on the set of a film. It was over a girl called Chloe Monkhurst. Clement had called Forrest a faggot and Bobby had punched him and continued to hit him once Clement was helpless. He had to be dragged away. At the time neither Forrest nor Clement was a big star, there were few people around and it wasn't too difficult to hush the matter up—a payment here, a promise there.

But Clement's injuries were far more serious than they thought. He needed several operations and these didn't go smoothly—complications, infections, nerve damage. The upshot was that Clement would never walk properly again and his face was disfigured. Like Michael Corleone in

The Godfather, he was left with a weeping eye and he also experienced breathing problems. This brought the insurance companies for the production outfit into play along with personal liability cover for the actors. As the one who'd arranged Bobby's liability insurance, Sophie was heavily involved in the assessments and arguments. In the end it came down to lawyers, threats of suits backwards and forwards and hefty payments to Clement.

The cover-up held as far as the public was concerned but some word got around among film people and casting agents steered clear of Bobby for a while. But he had a film in the can, one whose release was delayed for some reason, and when it was released he got good reviews and his star was on the rise. He got better and more varied parts, work in television and was on the brink of being a major figure when I met him.

Clement made threats against Bobby during the legal and financial negotiations. The documentation Sophie held ended with a copy of a statement signed by all the major parties pledging confidentiality as to the details of the settlement.

I worked through the rest of the material but the only thing of interest I found was a note from Bobby to Sophie telling her that he'd seen a psychiatrist at her suggestion and thought he might be some help with his problems. What problems? He didn't say. I knew that Sophie had been in therapy for years, so it would be natural for her to refer Bobby to her guy. I found him in Sophie's personal teledex—Dr Lucas

Kinsolving. I made copies of a few of the documents on Sophie's photocopier and tried to put the office back the way I'd found it. Sophie was still asleep, with her hand now tucked under her head. I put her keys back in her bag and left.

On the way home a memory kicked in: Chloe Monkhurst, who the fight between Bobby and Clement had been over and who'd been drunk and aggressive at the party, was the woman who'd given me the evil eye at Bobby's funeral.

I was energised and at the computer early the next morning. Dr Kinsolving was easy to find. He had consulting rooms in Bondi Junction and Chatswood—a both-sides-of-the-harbour guy—and he was an honorary member of staff of a couple of hospitals. He had a string of degrees and was the editor of a leading international journal of psychiatry.

There were a number of photographs of him posted. He was bald and bearded, impeccably dressed, and looked self-satisfied in shots of him in the company of distinguished people in the sciences and arts.

Jason Clement was more elusive. The few entries on him dated back in time and weren't much more than notices of his minor roles in minor films. He was a NIDA graduate and had briefly attended the Australian Institute of Sport as a hurdler before acting lured him away from athletics. A still from one of his film roles showed him as dark and passably good-looking. Back numbers of *Showcase*, the directory used by casting agencies to pick actors, was online and Clement appeared in two of the issues. He was represented by the Barton & Baird agency.

I phoned Barton & Baird and asked to speak to the agent who'd handled Jason Clement. There was a pause as the receptionist tapped keys.

'I'm sorry. We don't have a client of that name.'

'I know. He was on your books about four years ago.'

She sounded young. Four years probably seemed like a long time to her.

'Could you hold for a minute, please? I'll ask around.'

I waited, listening to music I couldn't identify.

'Are you there, sir? I think Tim Stafford might be able to help you.'

'Could I speak to him?'

'It's a she.'

'Tim is a she?'

'Her name is Timpani. I'm afraid not. She's out of town on location and won't be back for two days.'

'Could I have her mobile?'

'We don't give out numbers and anyway it wouldn't help, she's on a boat out at sea.'

'Is there no one else?'

'No. I'm sorry, I have calls waiting.'

I thanked her and said I'd ring again in a few days. Next I tried Dr Kinsolving but that was like picking your way through a minefield. I got an answering machine message at the Chatswood number advising me of the times the doctor would be in attendance. At the Bondi Junction number I actually got a living person but not much joy.

'You need a GP referral to see doctor,' the receptionist said.

'I'm not a patient. This is a different matter.'

'I can put you through to doctor's business manager.'

'I don't want his business manager, I want to speak to the doctor in person.'

'Doctor is very busy; if you're not a patient and it's not a business matter, I don't see . . .'

'Can you give him a message?'

'Of course.'

I told her I was a private detective employed by Ray Frost who was the father of Dr Kinsolving's client, the late Robert Forrest. I heard her gasp.

'Oh, Bobby.'

'Yes, Bobby. Tell the doctor it's very urgent that I speak with him.'

She was helpful now and took down my numbers and those for Ray Frost and said she'd get the message to doctor just as soon as she could. I wondered how long that would be but didn't press my luck by asking. I rang Ray Frost and told him a psychiatrist would be calling him to check on me.

'What psychiatrist?'

'Bobby's psychiatrist.'

'I didn't know he had one.'

'There's a few things about him we didn't know.'

'So you're still working on it. Are you getting anywhere?'

'Maybe.'

'Good. Stay with it and remember, any help you need I'm here.'

Kinsolving called an hour later and said he'd be happy to speak with me and he could give me some time at his Bondi Junction rooms at 2 pm that afternoon.

'Did you call Ray Frost?' I said.

'I had someone call him, yes.'

That's the way top people handle things. He sounded poised and confident and as if I should feel privileged to be talking to him in person. I hadn't met any of the people in Kinsolving's photo lineup, but then, he'd probably never met Brett Kirk or Jimmy Barnes. Remembering the doc's sartorial style, I wore the suit. I didn't think I'd need the gun.

Kinsolving's rooms were in a street close to the shopping centre but not too close. The street featured a row of elegant terrace houses with tiled porches reached by tiled paths and steps. Well-maintained iron fences, tasteful gardens, imposing teak doors. I mounted the steps and pressed the buzzer. A click told me a surveillance camera had taken a look at me. Then the door opened and I walked into a carpeted passage that smelled of money.

A discreet sign pointed me to a waiting room halfway

along the passage. Wide marble stairs with a polished hand-rail mounted to the heavens.

I went into the waiting room where a woman sat behind a desk. I agreed that I was Mr Hardy and she got up and opened a door. I went in to a large room with muted lighting. Bookshelves, a couple of armchairs, no desk, no couch. Dr Kinsolving came towards me with his hand out.

'Mr Hardy, so glad to meet you. Please sit down. Would you like anything—tea, coffee?'

'No thanks, doctor.'

I sat in one of the chairs. He remained standing for a few seconds—good manners or a little dominance strategy? He was about fifty, getting a bit portly but tall enough to carry it for a few years yet. His shirt and tie were blue, restful colours. His voice was quiet and his manner was confident.

'Never met anyone in your profession before,' he said as he sat. 'I imagine you're the sorts of fellows who can handle their own problems. Would you say?'

'Possibly. In my case, so far.'

'Good. Now I don't have a lot of time. How can I be of help? I have to warn you, the constraints on what I can say about a client are severe.'

'Even if he's dead?'

'Yes.'

'Can you tell me, in very general terms, what problem Bobby Forrest came to you with?'

'No.'

'I know he had sexual problems. He told me about them. I'm not interested in that. I'm wondering if he had . . . fears.'

He smiled. 'Sexual problems generate possibly the worst fears of all.'

'Okay. I'll be direct. I'm trying to find out who killed him. I've got a possible candidate but not much information on the circumstances. I've been told there was a person who threatened him. I'd like to know whether Bobby took the threat seriously.'

'I've never had a client murdered before. It's left me with a very uneasy feeling. I'm wondering whether I could have done more for him. Perhaps prevented this from happening.'

'You know, doctor, you're the fourth person to have that feeling.'

This didn't please him. His eyebrows shot up. 'Really, who?'

'His father, his girlfriend and me.'

'You've met her, the girlfriend?'

'Yes.'

'What's she like?'

'Very impressive, mature, intelligent . . .'

'Yes, I imagine so.'

He nodded as if he were talking to himself. He swivelled half away in his chair and seemed to be carrying on a silent dialogue with his eyes half closed and his hand stroking his beard. The silence didn't bother him. Eventually he swung back and faced me.

'I'm going to break some rules and be as frank with you as I can. Robert came to me with a troubling doubt about his sexuality. He had problems with impotence and wondered if he were homosexual. Obviously I can't tell you about the experiences he'd had that gave rise to this doubt. We talked about it of course, and also about other matters. To answer your question, yes, he was worried about the threat and took it very seriously.'

'Thank you. Why did you decide to be frank?'

'Your interesting description of the girlfriend. She must be a remarkable person. Robert was a different man after he met her. He acquired sexual confidence and this threat you've mentioned didn't seem to trouble him as much as it had. The change in him was extraordinary and I'm honest enough to admit it was more due to her than to me.'

I nodded.

'I can tell you a little more. Robert said he'd tried to make amends to the man who threatened him but didn't succeed. The man said he would kill him.'

19

Waiting for Timpani Stafford to return from wherever she was tried my patience. I hadn't got around to watching the DVDs of Bobby's films. Now I did, with a lot of fast forwarding. Bobby had style. The bonus was that Jason Clement had small parts, playing the sidekick to someone else in two of them. He didn't have a lot to do or much to say but he appeared to be perfectly competent. He also looked big and strong and moved like an athlete. They can't teach that at NIDA; it's a kind of gracefulness that some men have naturally, like Ali, like Carl Lewis, like Roger Federer. There was no interaction between Clement and Bobby in the films but I thought back to the driver Bobby had challenged at the lights. Like that guy, Clement was bigger than Bobby but I could see Bobby taking him on if his blood was up.

I arranged to have lunch with Jane Devereaux. She was getting on with her life as I was pretty sure she would. I'd checked with her a couple of times before and she'd said there'd been no approach of any kind from Michael Tennyson. But she had no interest in simply 'moving on' as the expression goes. She was anxious about the progress of my investigation, disappointed when there wasn't any, and keen to hear what I had to say now. We met in the Surry Hills wine bar again. The weather was warmer than before; she wore trousers, a sleeveless top and flat heels. Salads and garlic bread; white wine for me, mineral water for her.

'How's the book on the police chief going?' I asked.

'Just about ready. He was an interesting man. He had a network of informers, some of them quite as bad as the people they were informing on.'

'That'd be right.'

'D'you want to come to the launch?'

I said I would and then asked her if the name Jason Clement meant anything to her.

'Yes, Robert talked about him.'

'What did he say?'

She worked on her salad before answering. I knew what was going on. She'd compartmentalised her memories of Bobby and put them aside to allow her to function. Now she was opening the door. I ate and drank and gave her time.

'He told me he was his enemy. No, I haven't made that clear. He meant that Jason Clement regarded Robert as his enemy, but that Robert didn't regard *him* as an enemy. Do you follow? Why? What's happening?'

'Just a minute. Did he say why Clement felt like that?'

'No.'

'Didn't you ask him?'

'No. When it came up he seemed very disturbed about it. He changed the subject quickly and I could see it wasn't something he wanted to talk about. Do you know?'

I told her they'd had a fight but didn't go into the details. I said there was a possibility Clement was responsible for Bobby's death and that I was trying to find him. I wanted to know how seriously Bobby took the threat.

'I think he took it seriously. Did you know he was seeing a therapist?'

I nodded. 'Kinsolving.'

'No, just a therapist. He was helping him with anger management. Robert said he had a fierce temper but was learning to control it.'

'Do you know who this anger management therapist was?'

'No, he didn't say. I think he was a little ashamed of needing that kind of help. It just slipped out somehow when he was talking about golf. All I remember is that he said he mostly had the problem on the golf course. Can you find Clement, Cliff?'

I'd given up my 'no paper' policy and was scribbling some notes. 'I'll find him.'

'There's one thing I can tell you. It came up again briefly, and Robert said he'd seen Clement recently, but things were still the same.'

'How recently?'

She hadn't finished but she pushed the plate away, all appetite gone. 'Just before he died,' she said.

Clement had been locatable not so very long ago. I was encouraged, but the feeling didn't last long. I called Timpani Stafford and told her I was anxious to contact Jason Clement.

'So are we,' she said. 'We're holding some fees for residuals for him.'

'Money he's owed?'

'That's right. He's not at his last address and his mobile's been disconnected. His email bounces back. What's your interest?'

'Something the same. When was your last contact with him?'

'A couple of years ago.'

'How hard did you try?'

'I beg your pardon.'

'I'm sorry, it just seems strange that you wouldn't persist.'

'It was a small amount of money.'

'And Jason had got a big payout, right?'

'That's not something I'm prepared to discuss. If you find Jason, tell him we're anxious to hear from him.'

She hung up. Dead end. I was in my office with the copies of the documents I'd made in Sophie's office in front of me. I went over them again looking for leads but nothing emerged. The names of several lawyers who'd been involved in the negotiations and settlement were on record but the confidentiality provision would gag them forever.

I looked over the notes I'd written and saw Jane Devereaux's mention of Bobby's anger on the golf course. I'd heard enough about golf to know that anger is a problem for players at all levels. Maybe Bobby had mentioned his fight with Clement to his anger management guru. It was worth a try. I drove to the Anzac Park golf club and followed the sign to the pro shop. It was a quiet time and the guy in the shop looked bored as he rearranged packets of tees and boxes of balls on the counter. A golf tournament was playing on a TV set mounted on a wall where the pro could see it but he didn't seem very interested. I'd read that interest in golf had fallen away dramatically since the downfall of Tiger Woods.

'Afternoon,' I said.

'Gidday.'

I showed him my licence and told him I was working for Bobby Forrest's father, investigating Bobby's murder. That got his attention.

'Terrible thing,' he said.

'You knew Bobby?'

'Sure, he was a member here. Nice bloke, good player.'

'I believe he had some problems with anger while playing.'

'Yeah. You play?'

'No.'

'It gets to some blokes. Doesn't seem to happen to the women, but. Happens when blokes can't play as well as they think they should. We all feel like that really, but some people just can't cope with it.'

I nodded. 'I believe he was seeing a therapist to help with that.'

He laughed. 'I wouldn't call him a therapist. Calls himself an anger management consultant. I put Bobby on to him.'

'I'd like to talk to him. Can you give me his name?'

'Do better than that.' He rummaged under the counter and came up with a box of business cards. He flicked through and selected one. 'Here you go.'

The card read: *Barrie Monkhurst, Anger Management Consultant. Control your anger, improve your life.* It carried an address in Kogarah and a mobile phone number. I reached for my notebook and pen. *Monkhurst*, I thought. *Chloe's name. Not a common one. A coincidence or were connections starting?*

'You can keep the card, mate. I've got a few of them. Planning to see Barrie?'

'Yes, what can you tell me about him?'

'Well, he used to be a tour player but he wasn't quite good enough. Had a few pro jobs around the place but they never seemed to work out.'

'Why not?'

He laughed. 'Anger, why else? Barrie tells me he did a course in anger management that helped him and so now he helps others. Charges 'em pretty steep, but I reckoned Bobby could afford it.'

'Did it help Bobby?'

He shrugged. 'His handicap didn't come down.'

That's the trouble with golfers—they only have one way of measuring things. 'I meant did it help him with his temper?'

'Dunno. Didn't hear any complaints about him and our members are right down on that sort of stuff. One thrown club can bring on a suspension.'

My lawyer Viv Garner was a keen golfer who played to a low handicap in club competition until heart trouble reduced him to playing socially and using a cart, all of which he resented. I knew he kept up a keen interest in the sport. I rang him and asked if he'd ever heard of Barrie Monkhurst.

'Heard of him? I acted for him.'

'What was the charge?'

'Insurance fraud leading to assault. He was a pro at a golf club. He'd cooked the books to claim insurance money. When the assessor picked the dodge up Monkhurst bashed him. Put him in hospital.'

'What happened?'

'I got him a good barrister and he went to work. No one likes insurance companies and he got some juice out of that. He argued Monkhurst had anger management issues and was receiving counselling for it. A sympathetic magistrate let him off with a fairly hefty restitution order and a suspended sentence. He lost the job, of course, and they took that into consideration. But I'd be surprised if he ever made the restitution in full.'

'Why?'

'Monkhurst hired a member of my profession who's notorious for delaying settlements and restitution payments. He strings things out until all the other parties lose interest or settle for token amounts. He's a genius at it.'

'I'm shocked.'

'No you're not.'

'Did Monkhurst pay you?'

'After a time. I'm a persistent bugger and I had a good collector.'

'When was this?'

'Ten years ago. About then. Monkhurst's a dodgy character. I hope you're not relying on him for anything.'

'I'm not.'

'Good, because I can tell you that whatever he's doing now it won't be on the up and up.'

20

From the sound of things, it was smart to play it cagey with Monkhurst. I rang him.

'This is Barrie.'

'Mr Monkhurst, I've been referred to you by the pro at Anzac Park.'

'Steve, okay. Are you a golfer?'

'No. I was referred to Steve by someone else.'

'I get it. You have a problem with anger, ah, what's your name?'

'Cliff.'

'Problem with anger, Cliff?'

'That's right.'

'Is it to do with a sport or more generally?'

'Bit of both really.'

'Explain.'

'I do my block at squash sometimes and I experience road rage.'

'That's serious. That can get you into real trouble.'

'It already has.'

'I'm sure I can help you. I charge a hundred and twenty dollars for the initial consultation and there's a sliding scale of fees after that depending on how we attack the problem. You'll notice I say attack. That's an aggressive word. Does it surprise you that I use an aggressive word like that?'

'Um, well, yeah, a bit.'

'Don't let it worry you. Anger has to be beaten.'

'Right. The fees don't bother me.'

'What I like to hear. You know there's no Medicare rebate or anything like that?'

'I'm not worried. If I don't do something about this, my life's going down the toilet.'

'Can't let that happen, Cliff. When can you come and see me?'

'What's wrong with now?'

He laughed. 'That eager? All right, say in ninety minutes. I suppose Steve gave you my card so you know where I am.'

'Yeah, Kogarah. Ninety minutes is fine. Cash?'

'You bet. I'll be very angry if you haven't got it. That's a joke, Cliff.'

I laughed politely.

All I knew about Kogarah was that Clive James used to live there and run his billy cart down a hill. My business had never taken me there before and the closest I'd been was to Brighton-le-Sands to the east. Monkhurst's street ran parallel to the railway line and the house was closer to the tracks than I'd have wanted. Train noise in the middle distance is okay but you don't want it drowning out the television. The house was a cream-brick semi, neither shabby nor well looked after; the gate hinges needed oiling and the weeds were winning a battle against the grass.

I'd rehearsed my story. The only way to deal with a con man is to con him. I used the door knocker, hitting harder than I needed to. I heard footsteps inside and the door was opened by a man wearing a tracksuit and carrying a can of beer in his left hand.

He said, 'Cliff?'

I said, 'Right. Barrie?'

'That's me, come on in and have a beer. I hope you drink beer.'

We shook hands. He had big, golfer's hands, very strong.

'I drink *some* beers,' I said. 'Not all.'

'I've got Toohey's Old.'

'That'll do.'

I followed him down a narrow passage past a couple of rooms, through an eat-in kitchen and out to a built-in sunroom at the back. Sea grass matting, cane furniture. The yard beyond it was completely concreted with a Hill's hoist sitting in the middle. Monkhurst had taken a can of beer from the fridge as we went through the kitchen, and now

he threw it to me in a hard, underarm toss. I caught it, just.
It jarred my hand and I glared at him.

'You've got the look all right. Sit down, let's have a
chinwag.'

He was about fifty, middle-size, not fat but getting there
with flesh under his chin and soft bulk to his upper body. I
sat, opened the can, took a swig and pulled out my wallet.
I put a hundred and twenty dollars of Ray Frost's money on
the table beside my chair.

He touched his eyebrows. 'You've done some boxing.'

I nodded. 'Amateur.'

He drank some beer. 'Ex-cop?'

'No . . .'

'Ex-something.'

'Army.'

'You don't say much.'

'I thought I was here to listen.'

'Right. Listen and learn. I used to be like you. Thought
I was a hard case with the world against me.'

'Maybe it was.'

He shook his head. 'No, I was wrong. The world doesn't
give a fuck, one way or the other. Understand that and you've
made a start.'

It went on like that for a while. Monkhurst was glib,
parroting things he'd probably picked up from self-help
books. Some of it made sense, some didn't. When he started
mentioning group sessions and role playing I began to detect

a move towards his sliding scale of fees. I continued to keep my responses to a minimum, wondering how I could introduce the subject of Bobby Forrest.

Eventually I said, 'Any notable successes, Barrie? People I might have heard of?'

His eyes went shrewd and he hesitated. 'Well, I don't like to . . .'

Before he could finish the sentence the front door banged. A young woman came bustling into the house and headed down to the sunroom.

'Dad, I . . .'

She looked at me and her hand flew up to her mouth. She almost sagged against the door frame. 'What the fuck are you doing here?'

'Don't talk like that, Chloe. Sorry, Cliff, this is my daughter, Chloe. She's not usually so bloody rude. Chloe, this is a client, you shouldn't—'

'He's not a client, you idiot. He's that fucking private detective.'

She bore an unfortunate, heavy-featured resemblance to her father. Not drunk now, she was just as aggressive as at the Balmain party. She wore a tank top, jeans and boots. Her left arm was tattooed from the shoulder to the wrist. Her face was set in an angry scowl as she kicked one of Monkhurst's empty cans across the floor.

Monkhurst stared at me. 'Private detective? What . . .?'

'He's the one that was on TV when Bobby Forrest got killed. Don't talk to him, you dumb pisspot.'

Disrespect for a parent isn't uncommon but this was something much more than that. She was close to hysterical.

'That's me,' I said quietly. 'Why're you so upset?'

She glared at me and clenched her fist. 'You know, don't you, you fucker? You know!'

'Know what?' Monkhurst barked. 'What're you talking about?'

She glared at me as she pulled a mobile phone from her pocket. 'You'll never find him.'

'I'll find him.'

Monkhurst shook his empty can. 'Find who?'

'Make it easy on him, Chloe,' I said. 'Tell me where he is.'

'Easy! Nothing's easy. Fuck you!'

She ran from the room, down the passage. The door banged again. An engine started up and there was a roar as a car took off at speed.

Monkhurst crushed his beer can in those big hands. He glared at me.

'Private detective?'

'That's right.' I showed him my licence, taking care to keep out of his reach. Anger was building in him slowly but surely. His face was turning red and a vein in his forehead was throbbing.

'Calm down, Barrie. Your blood pressure's rising. I'm looking into the death of Bobby Forrest. He was my client like he was yours.'

'I ought to . . .'

'You shouldn't. I was punching people while you were practising your putting. You'd get hurt. Try some of your own medicine.'

'Fucking get out.'

'No chance. That daughter of yours is in trouble and you've got some explaining to do if you want me to keep the cops out of this.'

He went to the fridge and got himself another beer. He applied the cold can to his flushed face. He hadn't mentioned that particular anger management strategy. He threw himself down in the chair, opened the can and took a long pull.

'That girl'll be the death of me.'

He realised what he'd said and suddenly looked more worried than angry.

'I was leading up to asking you about Bobby.'

He shrugged. 'Poor bugger. What did Chloe mean by saying you know something? What d'you fucking know? I don't understand any of this.'

'I think she meant I know who killed Bobby. I don't. That's why you're going to talk to me about you and Bobby and everything about him you told Chloe.'

It took a while and more beer before I finally got it all from him. He'd gone through his usual routines with Bobby and claimed to have had some success.

'He was in a bad way with it. Hair-trigger temper, know what I mean? Like I used to have. He'd had this fight and hurt a bloke. Felt real guilty about it. Then he got better.'

'When?'

'Few months back.'

'You kept seeing him, though.'

'Yeah, I persuaded him he needed reinforcement sessions.'

'You're a con artist, Barrie.'

'It's legal.'

I was willing to bet that Bobby's improvement had more to do with Jane Devereaux than Monkhurst's games but I didn't say so. I didn't want to antagonise him any more than I had to.

'Okay, now how much about Bobby did you pass on to Chloe?'

'What do you mean?'

'Did you tell her about this business he felt guilty about?'

'Well, yeah, I suppose. We talked about it a bit. I mean, it's fucking hard to find anything to talk about with kids these days. They don't seem interested in sports or nothing. Chloe reckoned she was a fan of Bobby's. Watched him on telly and that.'

'Did he tell you who the fight was with?'

'Yeah, Clement somebody. He was real sorry about it. Came close to crying. Bit of a wuss.'

'Did you tell Chloe about Clement?'

'Yeah, she said she knew him. I told Bobby that and he wanted to talk to Chloe to see if she could get him together with Clement. But Chloe wouldn't even listen. Just laughed.'

'Did you tell Chloe where Bobby lived?'

'Dunno. I made some notes. She could've looked at them.'

'She saw his car?'

'Course she did. What's going on?'

'Here's the big question—do you know where Clement lives?'

'Wouldn't have a clue. Jesus, I get it. You reckon this Clement killed Bobby?'

'Could be. He was very badly hurt. It finished his acting career.'

'Fuckin' actors. Wankers. I remember now. That's where Chloe met Clement. She wants to be an actor. She goes to some acting classes and Clement's one of the teachers.'

'What classes? Where?'

'Don't know. I wasn't that interested.'

'Does Chloe have an address book?'

'Carries it around with her all the time. I think she's got most of that stuff in her phone anyway.'

'Does she keep a diary?'

'Not that I know of. Do people still do that?'

'I want to look in her room.'

'I'm not sure about that.'

'Look, if she passed on information to Clement and he killed Bobby, she's an accessory.'

'Shit.'

'I could try to keep her out of it.'

He nodded wearily. 'Second door. It'll be a mess.'

A mess was right. Chloe Monkhurst looked to be about twenty—if she hadn't decided to live tidily by now it was unlikely she ever would. She'd been wearing jeans and a tank top and there were similar items of clothing spread over the bed, the chest of drawers and lying on the floor. Shoes, too, and jackets. There was a snowstorm of used tissues and layers of magazines and CDs—some in their cases, some not.

A small table by the bed held a TV set with a DVD player and the discs were stacked beside it, like the CDs, in and out of their cases. No books. Would someone who lived in such chaos keep a diary? Hard to say.

We stood in the doorway. Monkhurst shook his head. 'Rather you than me.'

'What does she do?'

'Search me.'

'You must have some idea.'

'She sleeps and eats here, some of the time.'

I searched the room. I found condoms and roaches, unidentifiable pills and cards for a variety of businesses— body waxers, eyelash tinters, body piercers and a tanning studio. Under the bed was a Sargasso Sea of tights, socks, more tissues and underwear. There was no diary, but tucked in among the CD cases I found a brochure for the Newtown School of Acting.

YOU CAN ACT
LET US BRING OUT THE
CATE BLANCHETT &
HUGH JACKMAN IN YOU

The brochure advertised different kinds of classes for different levels, times and the qualifications of some of the teachers—their roles and brief notices on their performances. Jason Clement wasn't listed. The address was Angel Street, Newtown.

I took the brochure out to where Monkhurst was sitting with another can. I was thinking of taking him with me but he was too drunk.

'I want to ring her,' I said. 'What's her number?'

'Dunno. It's on my phone.'

'Ring her.'

'Why?'

'Just do it.'

He fumbled the phone from his pocket, peered at it and slowly punched in the numbers. He held it to his ear and shook his head.

'Disconnected.'

'What sort of car does she drive?'

'Volkswagen Beetle.'

'Colour?'

'Red.'

'Rego?'

'YZE something. Why d' you . . .'

'I might be able to talk some sense into her.'

He laughed. 'Forget it. She spotted you for what you are. Nothing but fucking trouble. Should've spotted it myself. Take your money and piss off.'

I put one of my cards on top of the notes. 'If she comes back or gets in touch tell her to ring me.'

'Why would she do that?'

'I don't want to cause her any trouble. I just want to know who killed Bobby Forrest.'

'And then do what?'

'I don't know. It could've been an accident. It needs talking about.'

He blinked, drunk but trying to get a grip on things.

'I reckon you're telling the truth.'

'That's right. If she's in with Jason Clement and he killed Forrest, I'm her best chance.'

21

Angel Street wasn't far from the office I used to have in Newtown. I'd handed it over to Hank Bachelor when I lost my licence. He still had it and I called in there before going to the acting school. It always pays to know what's going on in the precinct you're working in. As to the specific place you're heading for, it's useful to ask, as the cops do—anything known? Hank would have some idea.

He was there working on a piece of electronic equipment I'd never heard of designed to do something I didn't understand.

'Angel Street acting joint,' Hank said. 'Yeah, I know it. Struggling, I'd say. It's in an old warehouse, small one. Rent'd be high though and maintenance low. A couple of well-known actors have done stints there as teachers in its better days.'

'Any trouble?'

'There was something a while back. To do with firearms, I think, but I forget the details. And there was some sort of protest from parents about them trying to recruit directly from the Newtown Performing Arts High School in King Street. Fizzled out. What's your business there, Cliff?'

'Looking for a woman.'

He grinned. 'That's what Megan says you should be doing.'

'Is she still on about that?'

'Yeah, but I guess that's not what you have in mind. Do you need backup?'

'No, but I'll call you if I do.'

Angel Street is a block away from the main drag. It bends in the middle and part of it is blocked off to control the traffic flow. There's a playground-cum-park on one corner and on a couple of other corners there are houses that were once shops. Gentrification has gone a fair way but there are still some old houses in poor repair and buildings like the one the acting school occupied that have seen much better days. It was brick, two-storeyed, and rose directly up from the edge of the footpath.

I parked opposite and went through a battered double doorway and up a short flight of steps. The interior was brightly lit by artificial light. The windows were so small and dirty it would otherwise have been in perpetual gloom. The ground floor was a small auditorium—a tiny stage and about a dozen rows of chairs that looked as if they'd seen a lot of service somewhere else. A flight of stairs led up to the second level, where I could hear voices and physical activity. I went up and found an area that resembled a gym with some exercise equipment and mats on the floor. A partitioned-off area was divided into small offices.

About a dozen people were doing calisthenics guided by an instructor. There were five or six women but none of them was Chloe Monkhurst. I waited until the set of exercises was finished and the group was taking a break before approaching the instructor. I showed him my licence.

He picked up a towel from the floor and wiped himself down. The exercises had been vigorous and he wasn't young or in the very best physical condition.

'What's the trouble?' he said.

'No trouble. I'm looking for Chloe Monkhurst.'

'Not here.'

'I can see that. When is she here?'

He shrugged. 'Not that often.'

'How about Jason Clement?'

He shook his head and pointed to one of the offices. 'You'd better talk to the director. She's in there—Kylie March.'

Director seemed a bit elevated as a title for the head of the operation, and it was interesting that the first thing he'd done was ask about trouble. The would-be actors were a mixed bunch—some very young, some older; some scruffy, some well turned out. A few watched me closely. I hoped I was giving a good performance as a private investigator looking for information. I knocked on the door and opened it as a woman's voice invited me in.

Kylie March looked the part. She was about forty, rail-thin in a figure-flattering black top with black pants. She was heavily made up and no Caucasian ever had hair that black naturally. She was sitting cross-legged and sideways at a desk studying a laptop computer screen she'd moved around to get the right illumination. She tapped a couple of keys before looking up at me. A performance.

'Yes? Can I help you?'

I showed her my licence and told her who I was looking for. She asked me to sit but there was no chair.

'Silly me,' she said. Her voice was low and breathy.

'It's okay,' I said. 'I'll stand. I know where Chloe lives but it's Jason Clement I'm really looking for. I understand he works here.'

'He did. No longer.'

'Why is that?'

'Is he in trouble?'

'I believe so. How serious, is the question. That's why I need to talk to him. Do you know where I can find him?'

The screen went blank. She hit a key to bring it to life and then used the mouse to close it down.

'You can Google me if you want to,' I said, 'see that I'm legitimate.'

'Oh, I believe you're legitimate. I'm just wondering whether I should help you or not.'

'If you have Chloe and Jason's interests at heart you should.'

'I wouldn't say I had their interests at heart particularly. My concern is the school and I'm wondering whether your investigation will do it good or harm. I have a big investment here, you see, and I have to protect it.'

'That's honest,' I said, 'so I'll try to be equally honest. I can't say how things will work out. At best I don't think your school need come into it. If things go a different way it might, and I suppose it could come in for some . . . notoriety.'

'Notoriety isn't such a bad thing in this business, depending on how it's handled. May I have some time to think about it?'

'No. It's urgent and if you don't help me I'll have to come at it another way and then I wouldn't care much about the reputation of your school.'

'What other way?'

I took a punt. 'I'm told there was an incident here some time back. Something to do with firearms. I could look into that for a start.'

It hit the mark. She slammed the lid down on the computer, picked up its case from the floor and slid it in. She hooked a jacket and a shoulder bag from the back of her chair and stood.

'Okay, I'll talk to you. You can buy me a drink or a couple of drinks so I get something out of it at least.'

■ ■ ■

We sat in the bar of the Bank Hotel with the windows open and the life of Newtown swirling around us. Kylie March ordered a martini, saying that was what people in films drank when they talked with private detectives. I had white wine.

'How much do you know about Jason Clement?' she asked.

It's not best practice to let an informant ask the first question, but I had the feeling that Ms March would treat the interview like a performance and I might as well let her as long as I eventually got what I wanted. It was going to cost Ray Frost a bit—martinis don't come cheap.

'I know something,' I said. 'He was a promising actor and then something happened to him.'

'He was brilliant. He was in a class I ran at NIDA and he was far and away the best. He had the poise, the timing, *it*. You know what I mean by that?'

'I think so. A special quality. I've heard people say Cate Blanchett had it at NIDA.'

She nodded. 'She did, in spades. Jason had another aspect of the quality that's very important—an ability, sort of subliminal, to appeal to both sexes. He wasn't bisexual as far as I know, but there was something androgynous about him.'

'Like Elvis.'

'Before my time. Then he had an accident of some kind. He never said exactly what it was. I suspected a motorcycle accident.'

'Like Bob Dylan.'

She drained her glass and pushed it towards me. 'I'm not sure you're being serious.'

I got up. 'I am serious, Ms March, but I'm not much concerned about Clement's history. I just want to find him and I'll invest in another drink but my patience is running out.'

She didn't like it, but she didn't gather her things and leave. Probably holding on for a good exit line. The bar was crowded and I had to wait to be served. I kept an eye on her. She took a mobile phone from her bag and made a call. Hard to interpret that. I returned with the drinks.

'Thank you.'

'Take your time with the drink. I'm interested in why Clement left your school,' I said. 'I'd like to hear about the firearm incident.'

She was mollified and gave me a practised smile. 'Jason had all sorts of problems with his mobility and his appearance— even with his voice—but he was very brave about it. In his teaching he tended to take things to extremes.'

'For example?'

'He was a great one for things like Russian roulette. He pushed the students to the limits of their physical and emotional capacity. That was a good thing in a way, it sorted out the sheep from the goats.'

'Chloe Monkhurst?'

She worked on her drink, bleeding the moment for all it was worth. 'She couldn't stand the pace. She became a sort of acolyte, an assistant, rather than a student. Jason was a great one for reality and he went too far. He was demonstrating a shooting scene and he put live ammunition in the gun.'

'Pistol or rifle or shotgun?'

'Does it matter?'

'Maybe.'

'Pistol. A student was wounded. Only very slightly but he made a complaint. The police were involved.'

'They would be. What happened?'

'There were no charges laid. The student withdrew his complaint. I suspect Jason intimidated him. I haven't seen Jason since then.'

'It didn't make the papers.'

'We were lucky. A very big news story broke just at that time. I forget what it was, but it blotted out the . . . incident.'

'How long ago did all this happen?'

She'd finished her drink. She didn't eat the olives. She reached into her bag and took out a small notebook with a reproduction of the Penguin edition of *Wuthering Heights* as its cover and leafed through it.

'A few months ago.'

Around the time Bobby Forrest took up with Jane Devereaux and things began to look rosy.

'Where is he?'

She shrugged. 'All I can tell you is where he was then.'

22

Kylie March told me that Clement had a farm at Picton.

'A farm?'

'Well, some land at least. I don't know how much. He's not poor, you know. He got a payout after his accident. I remember him saying that Mel Gibson and Russell Crowe had farms, so why shouldn't he have one. He was being ironic, of course. He's very bitter about what happened to him. He was only part-time with us, you understand. I don't think he needed the money, which wasn't much.'

'What's the address?'

She consulted the notebook. 'Lot 12, Salisbury Road, Picton, but, as I say, that was when he first came to me for a position. That was some time ago.'

'It's a starting point. Thank you. What kind of car does he drive?'

'The questions you ask. I don't know about cars. Quite a big one. I remember that he had it modified to enable him to cope with his disability.'

'What colour?'

'Let me think. I only saw it once or twice. It was white, I believe, and dusty, I assume from driving from Picton. You will consider the school, won't you? I have been cooperative, haven't I?'

It was the middle of the afternoon but we were well into daylight saving and there'd be light for quite a few hours yet. I drove home, changed into my version of country clothes—jeans, T-shirt, boots, denim jacket—hunted out a map of the area to the west of Sydney and put the .38 in the pocket of the jacket. Picton was eighty kilometres away. It wasn't going to be a comfortable drive—commuter traffic for most of the way and into the setting sun at the end.

There wasn't any concrete evidence against Clement but he had the motive, the means (he was evidently familiar with guns) and the opportunity. I was putting it together in my head as I drove. Chloe Monkhurst could have told Clement that her father was dealing with Bobby Forrest. Monkhurst told his daughter things he shouldn't have about Forrest's state of mind. Chloe passes these things on to Clement—details of the car, movements, habits. Embittered anyway, Clement sees Forrest pulling his life together and kills him.

From tracking him in his last days, Clement knows that Forrest has hired me and sends me a text message after he's killed Forrest.

It hung together pretty well. Clement tells Chloe about me and she freaks when she sees that I've progressed to contacting her father. What's her next move? Most likely to get this very bad news to Clement. What's his likely reaction? Anybody's guess.

I stopped for petrol and was slowed down by a rainstorm that swept in to the south-west and made the road slippery so that traffic speed dropped to a crawl. A few kilometres of that and the rain eased off and most of the traffic took the road to Campbelltown. I activated the GPS and found my way to Salisbury Road. The lot numbers were clearly marked.

I drove slowly with things to worry about. Chloe had had plenty of time to alert Clement. She'd have guessed that the old Falcon parked near her father's place was mine. She'd have told Clement and he'd had time to do what? Run? Stand and fight? He was armed and he knew this territory the way I knew Glebe Point Road. Farmers have rifles and shotguns. I had a pistol with an effective range of not much more than fifteen metres.

It always amazes me how few animals there are in Australian paddocks. The drought was well and truly over and the land was green but there still weren't many sheep or cows in sight. But what do I know? Maybe they were off being shorn or slaughtered.

The Salisbury Road blocks appeared to be large, ten hectares or so. Did that suggest they were hobby farms, genuine concerns or tax dodges? Again, I didn't know. A few had no visible buildings, others had buildings at a distance from the road. Some of the buildings were screened off by trees.

I was moving slowly past Lot 10 when I heard the roar of a powerful engine. A big, dirty 4WD with a massive bull bar came hurtling at me from a track on the right. I accelerated and swerved but it hit the rear passenger door and spun me around. The seatbelt saved me, but I was jerked this way and that before the car came to a halt.

The 4WD was stopped where it had hit me. The driver's door opened and a tallish, slim young man got out. Jason Clement limped badly and his body was oddly twisted. He stood staring at me before he approached cautiously. A pistol hung from a lanyard around his neck. I tried to release the seatbelt to reach the gun in the glove compartment but it had jammed and I was strapped in tight. He saw that and didn't touch the pistol. He tried to open my door but it wouldn't give.

He made a winding motion and I lowered the window. It only came down halfway.

His voice was pleasant. 'You all right, Mr Hardy?'

I nodded.

He smiled. An actor's smile—full of warmth and work with the eyes. 'Good. I've got nothing against you.'

A strong whiff of alcohol came from him.

'I'm glad of that,' I said. 'How about helping me release this seatbelt.'

He shook his head. 'I don't think so. It's over now.'

'What is?'

He sighed and I could smell the rum. 'Everything.'

He was looking straight at me but I wasn't sure he was seeing me. I'd seen that fixed look before on the faces of people who didn't care what happened to them.

'It doesn't have to be like that.'

'Yes it does. Do you go to the movies, Mr Hardy?'

Keep him talking, I thought. 'Yes.'

'I feel . . . I feel as if I've been in a movie for a long time. Ever since Bobby . . .'

'It's not a movie. It's real. You need help, Jason.'

He was leaning against the car because he was drunk and because his body had betrayed him. 'It's not real,' he said. 'Nothing is real.'

He turned, stumbled. Almost fell and laughed as he regained his balance. He walked back to the 4WD. He turned and said something I couldn't hear. I'm no lip reader but I think he said two words—'the end'.

He climbed in awkwardly, one hand lifting his right leg, and made a series of movements to allow him to work the controls. He started the motor and drove off in the direction of his farm.

I was aching down my right side and my left arm and shoulder were numb. It took twenty minutes to restore the feeling, then it hurt and it was a centimetre by centimetre process to dig into my jeans pocket for my Swiss army knife. I sawed through the seatbelt and scrambled painfully across to the passenger door and out of the car. When I decided I could walk I got the gun from the glove box and limped in the direction Jason had taken.

Lot 12 provided an open view down a straight dirt and gravel road to a small farmhouse and a large shed. I headed for a point where a clump of trees fringed the property and I could see across flat, open ground to the buildings. The sky had cleared and the light was holding. There were three vehicles parked nearby—one white car, one red and the dusty 4WD.

There was a cool breeze. I struggled into my jacket and checked the pistol. There was no cover of any kind between the fence and buildings. With difficulty I parted the strands of barbed wire and stepped through. I felt very exposed as I walked across the rough ground, stopping from time to time to check for movement ahead. Nothing. A hundred metres from the house a drainage ditch I couldn't see from the road ran across the paddock. A little beyond that was a long, flat strip of land about twenty metres wide and running for at least a hundred metres to the south. Wheel marks showed on the closely mown grass. A runway of some kind.

I moved on until I reached the cars. The VW was old and rusty. I glanced inside and saw the same kind of chaos as in Chloe Monkhurst's bedroom. The white Commodore was dusty but well maintained. The driver's position was fitted with a hand throttle and a device to help with using the pedals. Same with the 4WD. There was a red paint smudge on the passenger-side bumper bar of the Commodore.

I moved cautiously towards the house. It was an old-style farmhouse, double-fronted with a tin roof and a bullnose verandah supported by sturdy posts. The roof was steeply pitched with two windows. There was no garden or ornamentation of any kind, but the porch and the surrounding area were tidy and swept clean. The front door was standing open but I worked my way around, crouching low as I passed the side windows with the pistol in my hand. No sounds from inside except something being rattled by the breeze.

The shed was several metres off to the right with a stand of paperbark trees affording it some shade. It faced the long runway. It had a skylight but no windows. Its double doors were open and a ride-on lawnmower stood just outside them. I approached it carefully. There was just enough light from the skylight to see a workbench, various bits of equipment and fuel drums inside, all in neat order. Nothing else.

I put the gun in my pocket and approached the back of the house. There was a lean-to with an ancient washing machine and a double cement tub. What used to be called a washhouse. Split wood was stacked in a box beside the back door. I went into the house; everything was clean and tidy and the door moved smoothly on oiled hinges. The kitchen was old style, with a linoleum floor, wood-burning stove, chip hot-water heater, a kerosene refrigerator and an enamel sink. An empty glass sat in the sink. I sniffed it. Rum.

I moved through the house, inspecting the two bedrooms and the sitting room. The bedrooms held double beds and old wardrobes and chests of drawers. The only signs of modernity were in the sitting room, where there was a home entertainment unit with a massive screen and shelves full of DVDs. Two large bookshelves were crammed with books, mostly to do with stage and screen. There were a few on gymnastics and diving. An old-fashioned drinks tray stood on a sideboard. It contained half-full bottles of dry sherry, brandy and whisky; the bottle of Bundaberg rum was empty.

The old house creaked around me and the rattling I'd heard from outside was louder and coming from upstairs, joined now with another noise. I paused and waited until I'd distinguished the two sounds: a blind flapping and human sobbing. With my stiff right leg protesting, I struggled up the narrow staircase and into the small room on the right of the landing.

Chloe Monkhurst sat on an upturned tea chest by the window. She was racked by sobs as she stared out the window.

'Chloe,' I said.

She turned towards me and a pistol in her shaking hand came up pointed straight at my chest.

23

I stopped in the doorway and leaned against the jamb.

'Put it down, Chloe.'

'I'll shoot you.'

'No you won't. The gun's too heavy. You can hardly hold it.'

She tried to hold the pistol steady with her other hand but her eyes were blurred by tears and she fumbled. I got to her in two strides and wrenched the gun away, exerting the minimum amount of force. It was a Glock automatic, fully loaded and quite weighty. I put it on the floor out of her reach and stood beside her. She'd stopped crying but her shoulders had slumped forward making her look small and vulnerable.

'Where's Jason, Chloe?' I said.

She didn't answer for what seemed like minutes but was probably only seconds. There was something so tragic in her manner that time seemed distorted. The window was open and the light was fading fast.

'You'll never catch him.'

'Why not? I've got this far.'

'Yes. I shouldn't have told him about you.'

I squatted beside her. 'You told him all about your father and Bobby Forrest, didn't you?'

Her eyes drifted down to a set of photographs she'd spread out on the floor in front of her. I'd noticed them when I'd put the gun down but now I bent to take a closer look. There were twelve, arranged in a semicircle. Jason Clement was the subject: Jason at the beach, Jason aiming a pistol, Jason in company with people I didn't recognise, and four or five of Jason with Chloe. In one he was kissing her tattooed arm, in others they were smiling together at the camera or at each other. In one he was on crutches. It struck me how young he looked and how fresh and open his smile was. In the group photo several of the others were turned towards him and their looks were admiring. Youth, good looks and charisma—a powerful combination.

Chloe moved her feet and destroyed the pattern of the photos. She reached down and flicked some of them over, the ones in which they were together and glowing. She sniffed and knuckled her eyes. I had some tissues in a pocket of my jacket and I gave them to her. She wiped her face and dropped the tissues on the floor as she'd done a thousand times before.

'I love him.'

'I understand that. So when Jason found out all about Bobby and how he was happy and everything, he couldn't stand it and he killed him.'

'He'd had his life ruined. He had the right.'

'No, he didn't.'

'He used to be so good-looking and he could do everything and now he can't even . . .'

'He's got some sort of plane, hasn't he?'

She nodded. 'An ultra-light.'

'Where's he going?'

'Nowhere.'

'You're not making sense. I'm not trying to destroy him. Maybe it was an accident. It doesn't have to be the end of his life.'

She shook her head and seemed unable to speak. Then she pointed to the pistol. 'I told him to throw it away but he wouldn't.'

'What happened when you told him I'd been talking to your father?'

'He said he knew you'd catch up with him sooner or later. You or the police. He said he didn't care. He didn't care that I loved him. He didn't believe me.'

'That's hard.'

'He gave me a test. He said if I loved him I should go with him in the plane. I wanted to but I was too scared. I couldn't do it. So he laughed and said it couldn't be much of a love.'

'Why were you scared? Had you ever been in the plane before?'

'Yes, of course. You don't understand. He drank nearly a whole bottle of rum and he left the gun so you or the police would be able to prove what he'd done. He got the plane out of the shed. He said he had enough fuel for an hour's flying and that he planned to be a thousand feet up when it ran out.'

'How long ago was that?'

'I don't know. It feels like a long time. I didn't have the guts to go with him. He said I'd see him come down and be able to say goodbye.'

She started crying again as a distant buzzing sound grew louder and closer.

I retrieved the Glock and went downstairs and outside to stand at the top of the runway. I knew nothing at all about ultra-lights. Could they glide when the fuel ran out or did they drop like a stone? Was Clement serious about suicide, or would he change his mind or lose his nerve and land safely?

The sky was dark now but as the buzzing noise drew closer and became louder I could see a moving light high above. How high I had no idea—five hundred feet, a thousand feet? High enough anyway not to want to fall from. I looked back at the house and saw Chloe standing at the window watching the moving light.

The engine noise intensified as the plane swooped low over the house. It was painted white and just visible against the clouds. Then it climbed up towards the darkness and began a series of high, slow-seeming circuits above the property. It maintained or increased the height with each circuit and showed no signs of making an approach to the runway. With the light almost gone, it was doubtful that the pilot would be able to see the landing strip, and the ground to either side of it was rough and uneven.

Suddenly the engine noise changed into a sputtering whine that carried down to me on the breeze. I knew I was about to witness the death of another young person, the end of a life scarcely begun, and the realisation was like a heavy weight on my shoulders.

The light appeared to hang in the air for a second and then it went out. I lost sight of the plane and then picked it up again as it fell, turning end over end like a bird shot on the wing. The plane landed on the roof of the shed with a shattering sound as the skylight broke. Then there was an explosion and a sheet of flame as the shed burst apart at the seams.

I was too close and the blast knocked me flat as I heard Chloe's scream.

24

I rolled away from the blast and the heat and heard several more explosions. When I got to my feet I saw the skeleton of the place glowing red hot. The wooden parts of the shed were burning fiercely and the paperbarks were burning like torches.

I staggered back to the house and sat on the steps. Chloe appeared beside me. I moved to give her room and put my arm around her shoulders. She wasn't crying.

'He really did it,' she said.

'Yes. You were right not to go with him.'

She sighed and when she spoke her voice sounded older than before. 'I suppose so. Look, I need a smoke. I've got some dope in my car. You won't stop me, will you?'

'No, but better be quick. That fire's going to attract a lot of attention.'

She went to her car, treading gingerly barefoot on the

rough ground. She opened it, reached into the glove box and rolled a very big joint. She held it up inquiringly. I shook my head. She lit up and stood, smoking and watching the fire. She finished the joint and came back to tuck the stash under the steps. We sat there while the wood smouldered and the trees burned and shot sparks into the sky until we heard the sirens.

She rubbed at a fresh-looking tattoo on her right forearm. 'What will I say?'

'Tell them the truth.'

'That I helped Jason kill Bobby Forrest.'

'I wouldn't put it quite like that.'

'I did, you know,' she said and she went back into the house. I followed her but she'd gone upstairs. The sirens were close now and I thought I should be on the spot. I looked longingly at the drinks tray but thought better of it. I put the Glock on the sideboard and went out to meet them.

The police, an ambulance and the fire brigade arrived. I talked to them at the scene and several times later, along with someone from the Department of Civil Aviation. I was permitted to drive myself back to the city, but Chloe went in the ambulance. She was sobbing again, almost hysterical. Maybe she had acting talent after all.

What took place at police headquarters subsequently they called debriefing. It felt more like the kind of spray football coaches direct at poorly performing players. The Glock had fired the bullet that killed Bobby Forrest and the paint on the Commodore's bumper bar matched that on the Alfa Romeo.

I told Sean Rockwell he should be pleased the case was closed.

'You should've come to us.'

'With what? I had nothing solid.'

'I'd have listened to your suspicions and your reasoning.'

'Would you? I'll bear that in mind next time. Face it, Inspector, you're a busy man with a lot of things on your plate. This was all I had to think about and that's the difference.'

He gave me a weary smile. He wasn't a bad bloke. 'I bet you didn't even get the Falcon fixed,' he said.

The media gave it a big splash but such things have a brief time in the sun and it wasn't long before the story was displaced by others. I resisted all the offers and approaches for interviews. I didn't follow the coverage closely, but I didn't see any mention of the Newtown acting school, so Kylie March would be happy. Or maybe not. I remembered what she'd said about the value of managed notoriety.

I could certainly do without it and I took a short holiday in the Illawarra. I stayed in the Thirroul motel where Brett Whiteley had died but I scarcely spent any time there. I met Sarah on the evening I arrived and we ate and drank and walked on the beach and made love on a mattress on the deck of her house with the waves just audible when we stopped panting and laughing. We body-surfed at Thirroul beach, ate in the cafés and pubs that provide good food and service that help to keep the area going now that the coal mines have closed and the heavy industry has mostly shut down. We watched the hang-gliders who took off from Stanwell Tops and drifted and swooped far out to sea. The sight of them reawakened a query that had lodged somewhere in my mind but in the heat of our reunion I couldn't bring it into focus. She sang; I loved her voice. We swapped stories; it was all good, but she was Illawarra and I was Sydney. They weren't so far apart and we thought we could see a kind of future for us.

When I got back I set up a meeting with Ray Frost and Jane Devereaux. It was sad, but it went well. We said we'd stay in touch but we haven't. At Jane's invitation I went to the launch of Harry Tickener's book, *The Whole Truth*. There were a lot of media people there but not Michael Tennyson. The tape I had was insurance for Jane and for me and I wondered how long I should keep it and what I should do with it eventually. It was an uncomfortable feeling.

I haven't heard anything since about Chloe Monkhurst but I keep expecting to. There were no proceedings against her but I couldn't help wondering what she'd meant when she said: *'I did, you know.'* She was stoned when she said it but not totally stoned.

The questions the hang-gliders, men and women, had prompted me to ask myself as they soared above the Tasman

Sea were these: how disabled was Jason Clement? How competent or otherwise was he with firearms? He had had misadventures with guns before. Had Chloe really been in the car with him or was she as deluded and obsessed about Jason as he was about Bobby Forrest? I didn't know, and although it niggled at me, I didn't want to know.